Mrs. Molesworth

An Enchanted Garden

Fairy stories

Mrs. Molesworth

An Enchanted Garden
Fairy stories

ISBN/EAN: 9783337244323

Printed in Europe, USA, Canada, Australia, Japan

Cover: Foto ©Andreas Hilbeck / pixelio.de

More available books at **www.hansebooks.com**

AN ENCHANTED GARDEN

THE CHILDREN'S LIBRARY.

(Others in the Press.)

AN

ENCHANTED GARDEN

Fairy Stories

BY

MRS. MOLESWORTH

AUTHOR OF 'CARROTS,' 'THE CUCKOO CLOCK,
'THE PALACE IN THE GARDEN,' 'FIVE
MINUTES STORIES,' ETC.

ILLUSTRATED BY W. J. HENNESSY

LONDON
T. FISHER UNWIN
1892

TO

HENRY & DOROTHY WALTHALL

19 SUMNER PLACE, S.W.,
    9th March 1892.

CONTENTS

CHAPTER I

MADAM WREN

'NO,' said Alix, 'that's not a good plan at all. It's perfectly stupid. If you've no better ideas than that, Rafe, we needn't talk about it any more.'

Rafe looked and felt very snubbed indeed.

He was ten, she was nine. But she generally took the lead; not always, as I daresay you will see when you hear more about them, but *generally*. They were a nice little pair, and they were constantly together, at lessons, at play,

at everything.   This was a convenient
arrangement, for they were a good deal
younger than the other brothers and
sisters of the family, and what Rafe
would have been without Alix, or Alix
without Rafe, it would be difficult
to imagine.   But there is not much
use in thinking over about might-have-
beens, or would-have-beens, unless to
make us more thankful for what *is*.
So it is enough to say that as things
really were, they were very happy
children.

Still they had their troubles, and it
was one of these they were discussing
this lovely spring morning, when they
were sitting under their favourite tree
—a magnificent ilex in the garden, at
one corner of the great lawn which
was one of the beauties of their home.

It was a lovely day, clear and bright
and joyous, full of its own delights, and
yet almost fuller of the summer ones
to come !   This is, I suppose, the real
secret of the charm of spring-time—

the promise and hope it tells of. Everything seemed bursting with good news,
the birds most of all perhaps, though
the smiling faces of the early flowers,
and the tender whispers of the gentle
wind through the branches, were not
behindhand.　But the children's faces
were clouded.

This was their trouble.　They could
not get any one to tell them any more
stories !　They had read all their books
through, over and over again, and besides, books aren't *quite* as nice as
'told' stories.　At least not when they
have to be shared by two.　Rafe and
Alix had tried several plans—reading
aloud did not answer *very* well, and
looking over the pages was worse.
They never managed to keep quite
together, and then the one who got
down to the last line first was sure to
fidget or to try in some way to hurry
up the other, which was apt to lead to
unpleasant results.　And besides this,
at present there was no question of

story-books, for, as I said, the children
had read all they possessed really *too*
often.

Hitherto perhaps they had been a
little spoilt about having stories told
to them.   Papa, who was an old soldier,
had a good many tales of adventure ;
mamma had some lovely ones about
'when she was a little girl.'   And the
big brothers and sisters were very kind
too, especially if Rafe or Alix, or both,
as sometimes was the case, happened
to be ill.   But their stories were mostly
out of books ; now and then indeed
they would unluckily turn out to be
already known to the children, and
though they did not altogether object
to them on this account—I have noticed
that children rather enjoy a book story
retold by voice—it was not always so
pleasant for Ena or Jean, or Eric when
he was at home from college.   For Rafe
and Alix were so exceedingly particular.

'No,' one of them would say, just
when Eric had got to the most thrilling

part of a robber story, 'the entrance
to the inner cave was at the *left* side
of the big one;' or if Jean was de-
scribing her heroine's dress, 'It wasn't
green—I'm sure it was blue—blue
with tiny rosebuds on,' so that sometimes Jean would reply, 'Really, children, if you interrupt so I can't go on,'
or Eric would go off with a grunt and
tell them to provide stories for themselves.

This had happened the evening before, and this it was which put the idea
into Rafe's mind which Alix snubbed so.

'Suppose,' he said, 'that we make
stories for each other—you for me,
Alix, and I for you?'

It sounded rather nice, but it did
not find favour in her eyes at all.

'I know exactly what they'd be,' she
said; 'just mixings up of all our other
ones. It might do to amuse stranger
children with, perhaps—but not for us
ourselves. I know all that's in your
head, and you know what's in mine, far

too well. So it would be perfectly stupid.'

And Rafe had no more to say.

It was Easter holidays—Easter was as late as it could be that year—and the weather was so beautiful that it really felt like summer. You would think the children should have been content ; but they weren't. They had no lessons at all to do, and a whole fortnight of nothing you really must do is, in my opinion, a mistake. During the long summer holidays Miss Brander, their governess, always left them *something* to do, just enough to give a nice fresh taste to the holidaying the rest of their time, and to prevent their feeling the reins *quite* loose on their necks like runaway ponies. And even without this, in the summer it was different, for they generally went to the seaside or to some hilly place for a month or so, to have a change of air, and away from home in a new place time seldom hangs much on children's hands.

This Easter it was certainly doing
so a good deal. There were other
reasons too why the little couple felt
rather at a loose end, rather tired of
themselves. The big people were all
unusually busy, for Ena was going to
be married in June ; and she and their
mother or she and Jean were always
going somewhere or other to order
things, or to give their opinion about
the doing up of the pretty old house, ten
miles or so away, which was to be her
new home. And though Ena was very
kind when she had time, and the new
brother-to-be held out grand promises
of the visits they were to pay to their
sister, and the fun they should have,
still, all that seemed a good way off,
and in the meantime Rafe and Alix
felt rather out of it all. I am not sure
but that they were just a little jealous
of the new brother. 'It's only a pre-
tence sort of brother,' said Alix one day
when her feelings had been ruffled. I
am afraid they felt as if he had some-

how put both their small noses out of joint.

So now you understand why Rafe and Alix were sitting rather disconsolately under the ilex, though the sun was shining brightly enough to melt away all clouds and mists inside as well as outside, any one would have thought.

In spite of Alix's snub, Rafe looked up again in a minute or two.

'Why don't you think of a better plan, then, if you don't like mine?' he said. 'It's always easy to say things won't do' (which is exceedingly true!), 'but why don't you find something that *will* do?'

Alix turned round. She was sitting on the end of the rustic bench, swinging her legs, which was not difficult, as they scarcely reached the ground, and staring up at the thickly-growing branches overhead. But now she looked at Rafe—he felt a little nervous; was she going to take offence at his speech?

No—she had heard what he said, but she was not vexed.

'I know what I wish we *could* find,' she said. 'Do you remember, Rafe, the story of a white lady, up, up in a room at the very top of a castle some-where, who was always spinning stories? They came out of the hum of her spinning-wheel somehow, and the children could hear them when they sat down on the floor beside her. *Oh*, if we could find somebody like that!'

'It was fairies,' said Rafe doubt-fully. 'At least the white lady was a fairy, and there aren't any really, I suppose.'

'Everybody says so,' Alix replied doubtfully, 'but I don't quite see why there mightn't be. If there have never been any, what began all the fairy stories? And I know one thing— papa said so himself one day when he was telling some — what's the word?—it means a sort of a fairy story that's been told over and over

since ever, *ever* so long ago, ledge—
what is it?'

'Legends, you mean,' said her
brother. 'Yes, I remember papa
telling us some very queer ones he
had heard in India.'

'And he said there were fairy stories
in *every* country,' Alix went on. 'So
what *I* say is there must have been
something to make them begin!'

This sounded very convincing to
Rafe—Alix certainly had clever ways
of putting things.

'Oh!' he said, with a deep sigh.
'If we could but find some one old
enough to remember the beginnings of
them—something like the white lady,
you know.'

Both children sat silent for a moment
or two, their eyes gazing before them.
Suddenly on the short green turf appeared a tiny figure, a wren, so tame
that she hopped fearlessly to within a
very short distance of the little brother
and sister, and then, standing still,

seemed to look up at them with her bright eyes, her small head cocked knowingly on one side.

'Rafe,' exclaimed Alix eagerly, though in a low voice.

'Alix,' said Rafe in his turn.

Then they looked at each other, thinking the same thoughts.

'Rafe,' whispered Alix, while the wren still stood there looking at them, 'just look at her ; she's not a bird, she's a fairy—or at least if she's not a fairy she's got some message for us from one.'

The wren hopped on a few steps, still looking back at them. The children slipped off the seat and moved softly after her without speaking. On she went, hopping, then fluttering just a little way above the ground, then hopping again, till in this way she had led them right across the wide stretch of lawn to some shrubberies at the far side. Here a small footpath, scarcely visible till you were close to it, led through the bushes to a strip of half-wild garden ground, used as a sort of nursery for young trees, which skirted a lane known by the name of the 'Ladywood Path.' And indeed it was little more than a path nowadays, for few passed that way, though the story went that in the old days it had been a good road leading to a house that was no longer in existence.

Over the low wall clambered the children, to find to their delight that the wren was in the lane before them, just a little way ahead. But now she took to flying higher and faster than she had yet done ; to keep up with her at all they had to run, and even with this they sometimes lost sight of her altogether for a minute or two. But they kept up bravely—they were too eager and excited to waste breath by speaking. The race lasted for some minutes, till at last, just as Alix was about to give in, Rafe suddenly twitched her arm.

'Stop, Alix,' he panted—truth to

tell, the running was harder on him than on his sister, for Rafe was of an easy-going disposition, and not given to violent exercise—'stop, Alix, she's lighted on the old gateway.'

They both stood still and looked. Yes, there was Madam Wren on the topmost bar of a dilapidated wooden gate, standing between two solid posts at what had once been the entrance to the beautiful garden of an ancient house.

How beautiful neither the children nor any one now living knew, for even the very oldest inhabitants of that part of the country could only dimly remember having been told by their grandparents, or great-grandparents perhaps, how once upon a time Lady-wood Hall had been the pride of the neighbourhood.

The wren flapped her wings, then rose upwards and flew off. This time, somehow, the children felt that it was no use trying to follow her.

'She's gone for good,' said Rafe dolefully; but Alix's eyes sparkled.

'You *are* stupid,' she said. 'Don't you see what she's told us. We're to look for—for something, or some one, I don't quite know what, in the Lady's garden.' For so somehow the grounds of the vanished house had come to be spoken of. 'I think it was very dull of us not to have thought of it for ourselves, for it is a very fairy sort of place.'

'If it is that way,' said Rafe, '*they* must have heard us talking, and sent the wren to tell us.'

'Of course,' said Alix, 'that's just what I mean. Perhaps the wren is one herself.'

'Shall we go on now?' said Rafe. 'No'—for just at that moment the clear sound of a bell ringing reached them from the direction of their own home—'for there's our dinner.' And dinner was an important event in Rafe's eyes, even when rivalled by a fairy hunt.

'How provoking,' said Alix. '*How* quickly the morning has gone. We must go in now or they will come hunting us up and find out all about it ; and you know, Rafe, if it has anything to do with fairies we must keep it a secret.'

Rafe nodded his head sagely.

'Of course,' he replied. 'When do you think we had best come? This afternoon we are going a walk with nurse, and she'd never let us off.'

'No,' said Alix, with a sigh, for a walk with nurse was not a very interesting affair. 'But I'll tell you what, Rafe ; if I can get hold of mamma to-night, just even for a minute, I'll ask her if we mayn't take something for dinner out with us to-morrow, and not come in till tea-time — the way we sometimes did last summer ; for just now it's really as fine and warm as if it was June. I think she'll let us.'

'I do hope she will,' said the boy.

CHAPTER II

TAPPING

THE children were not very
fortunate in their nurse.
Perhaps this helped to
make them feel lonely and
dull sometimes, when there scarcely
seemed real reason for their being so.
She was a good woman, and meant to
be kind, and their mother trusted her
completely. But she was getting old,
and was rather tired of children. She
had had such a lot to bring up—the
four big brothers and sisters of Rafe
and Alix, and before them a large
family of their cousins. And I don't

think she was really very fond of children, though she was devoted to tiny babies. She didn't in the least understand children's fancifulnesses or many of their little ways, and was far too fond of saying, 'Stuff and nonsense, Master Rafe,' or 'Miss Alix,' as the case might be.

The walk this afternoon would not have been any livelier than usual, so far as nurse was concerned, but the children were so brimful of their new ideas that they felt quite bright and happy, and after a while even nurse was won over to enter into their talk, or at least to answer their questions pretty cheerfully.

For though of course they had not the least idea of telling her their secret, it was too much on their minds for them not to chatter round about it, so to say.

'Have you ever seen a fairy, nurse?' said Alix; and, rather to her surprise, nurse answered quite seriously:

'No, my dear. Time was, I suppose,

c

as such things were to be seen, but that's past and gone. People have to work too hard nowadays to give any thought to fairies or fairyland.'

But on the whole this reply was rather encouraging.

'You must have heard of fairies, though,' said Rafe. 'Can't you remember any stories about them?'

Nurse had never been great at story-telling.

'Oh dear no, Master Rafe,' she replied; 'I never knew any except the regular old ones, that you've got far prettier in your books than I could tell them. *Sayings* I may have heard, just country-side talk, when I was a child. My old granny, who lived and died in the village here, would have it that, for those that cared to look for them, there were odd sights and sounds in the grounds of the old house down the lane. Beautiful singing *her* mother had heard there when she was a girl; and once when a cow strayed

in there for a night, they said when
she came out again she was twice the
cow she had been before, and that
no milk was ever as good as hers.'

The children looked at each other.

'I wonder they didn't turn all the
cows in there,' said Rafe practically.
'Why didn't they, nurse?'

'Oh dear me, Master Rafe, that's
more than I can tell. It was but
an old tale. You can't expect much
sense in such.'

'Whom did the old house belong
to? Who lived there?' said Alix.

'Nobody knows,' said nurse. 'It's
too long ago to say. But there's
always been good luck about the place,
that's certain. You've seen the flowers
there in the summer time. Some of
them look as beautiful as if they were
in a proper garden; and it's certain
sure there's no wood near here like it
for the nightingales.'

This was very satisfactory so far as
it went, but nurse would say no more,

doubtless because she had nothing more to say.

'I do believe, Rafe,' said Alix, when they were sitting together after tea, 'that the old garden is a sort of entrance to fairyland, and that it's been waiting for us to find it out.'

Her eyes were shining with eagerness, and Rafe, too, felt very excited.

'I do hope mamma will let us have all to-morrow to ourselves,' he said. 'You see, one has to be very careful with fairies, Alix—all the stories agree about that. We must go to work very cautiously, so as not to offend them in any way.'

'You're always cautious,' said Alix, with a little contempt; 'rather too cautious for me. Of course we shall be very *polite*, and take care not to spoil any of the plants, but we'll have to be a little venturesome too. And,' she went on, 'you may count that they've invited us. The wren brought a regular message. I only hope they're not offended with us for not going to-day.'

' If they're good kind of fairies,' said Rafe sagely—'and I think they're sure to be—they wouldn't have liked us to be disobedient ; and you know mamma's awfully particular about our coming in the moment we hear the bell ring.'

' Yes,' said Alix ; 'that's true.'

Mamma's heart was extra soft that evening, I think. She had seen so little of the children lately that she was feeling rather sorry for them, and all the more ready to agree to any wish of theirs. So they had no difficulty in getting her consent to their picnic plan for to-morrow. And the weather was wonderfully settled, as it sometimes is even in England, though early in the year.

So the next morning saw them set off, carrying a little basket of provisions and a large parasol, full of eagerness and excitement as to what might be before them.

They did not cross the lawn as they
had done the day before, for they
had a sort of feeling that they did not
wish any one to see them start, or to
know exactly which way they went.   It
added to the pleasant mystery of the
expedition.   So they went straight out
by the front gates, and after following
the high road for a quarter of a mile
or so, entered a little wood which
skirted the grass-grown lane along one
side, and from which they made their
way out with some scrambling and
clambering at only a few yards' distance from the entrance to the deserted
garden where they had last seen the
wren.

The sight of the gate-posts reminded
Alix of the bird, and she stopped short
with some misgiving.

'Rafe,' she said, 'do you think perhaps we should have waited for her at
the ilex tree?   I never thought of it
before.'

'Oh no,' said Rafe; 'I'm sure it's

all right. We've come to the place
she led us to. She didn't need to
show us the way twice ! Fairies don't
like stupid people.'

'You seem to know a great lot
about fairies,' said Alix, who had no
idea of being snubbed herself, though
she was fond of snubbing other people;
'so I think you'd better settle what
we're to do.'

'I expect we'll find the wren inside
the gate,' said Rafe ; and they made
their way on in silence.

There was no difficulty in getting
into the grounds, for though the gate
on its rusty hinges would have been
far too heavy for the children to move,
there was a space between it and the
posts where the wood had rotted away,
through which it was easy for them
to creep. First came Rafe, then the
basket, next Alix, and finally the big
parasol.

It was a good while since they had
been in the Ladywood garden, and

when they had got on to their feet
again, they stood still for a minute or
two looking round them.   It was a
curious - looking place certainly;   the
very beauty of it had something strange
and dream-like about it.

Here and there the old paths were
clearly to be traced.   The main approach, or drive, as we should now
call it, leading to where the house had
been, was still quite distinct, though
the house itself was entirely gone—not
even any remains of ruins were to be
seen, for all the stone and wood of
which it had been built had long
since been carted away to be used
elsewhere.

But the children knew where the
old hall had actually stood—a large,
square, level plateau, bordered on three
sides by a broad terrace, all grass-
grown, showing in two or three places
where stone steps had once led down
to the lower grounds, told its own tale.
Along the front of this plateau, sup-

porting it, as it were, there was still a very strongly-built stone wall banked up into the soil. The children walked on slowly till they were near the foot of this wall, and then stood still again. It was about five feet high; they seemed attracted to it, they scarcely knew why—perhaps because it was the only remaining thing actually to show that here had been once a home where people had lived.

'I daresay,' said Alix, looking up, 'that the children used to run along the terrace at the top of that wall, and their mammas and nurses would call after them to take care they didn't fall over. Doesn't it seem funny, Rafe, to think there have *always* been children in the world?'

'I daresay the boys jumped down sometimes,' said Rafe. 'I'd like to try, but I won't to-day, for I promised mamma to take care of you, and if I sprained my ankle it would be rather awkward.'

They had forgotten their little quarrel, and for the moment they had forgotten about the wren.

She was nowhere to be seen.

What was to be done?

'If we were only looking for a nice place for our picnic,' said Rafe, 'nothing could be better than the shelter of this wall. With it on one side, and the parasol tilted up on the other, it would be as good as a tent.'

'But we're not only looking for a picnic place,' said Alix impatiently. 'The only thing to do is to poke about till we find *something*, for I'm perfectly certain the wren didn't bring us here for nothing; and then, you know, there's even what nurse told us about this garden.'

Alix's words roused Rafe's energy again; for he was a trifle lazy, and wouldn't have been altogether disinclined to sit down comfortably and think about dinner. But once he got a thing in his head, he was not without ideas.

'Let's follow right along the wall,' he said, 'and examine it closely.'

'I don't know what you expect to find,' said Alix. 'It's just a wall, as straight and plain as can be.'

And so indeed it seemed from where they stood.

'*I'll* look all along the ground, in case there might be a ring fixed in a stone somewhere, like in the *Arabian Nights*. That's a regular fairy sort of plan,' said Alix.

'Very well,' agreed Rafe; 'you can do that, and I'll keep tapping the wall to see if it sounds hollow anywhere.'

And so they proceeded, Alix carrying the basket now, and Rafe the parasol, as it came in handy for his tapping.

For some moments neither of them spoke. Alix's eyes were fixed on the ground. Once or twice, where it looked rough and uneven, she stooped to examine it more closely, but nothing came of it, except a little grumbling from Rafe at her stopping the way. To avoid this she ran on a few paces in front of him, so that when, within a few yards of the end of the wall, her brother suddenly stopped short, she wasn't aware that he had done so till she heard him calling her in a low but eager voice.

'What is it?' she said breathlessly, hurrying back again.

'Alix,' he said, 'there's some one tapping back at us from the other side. Listen.'

'A woodpecker,' said Alix hastily; 'or the echo of your tappings.'

She was in such a hurry that she didn't stop to reflect what silly things she was saying. To tell the truth, she didn't quite like the idea of Rafe having the honour and glory of the discovery, if such it was.

'A woodpecker,' repeated Rafe.

'What nonsense! Do woodpeckers tap inside a wall? And an echo wouldn't wait till I had finished tapping to begin. It's just like answering me. Listen again.'

He tapped three times, slowly and distinctly, then stopped. Yes, sure enough there came what seemed indeed like an answer. Three clear, sharp little raps—clearer and sharper, indeed, than those he made with the parasol handle. Alix was now quite convinced.

'It sounds like a little silver hammer,' she said. 'Oh, Rafe, *suppose* we've really found something magic!' and her bright eyes danced with eagerness.

Rafe did not reply. He seemed intent on listening.

'Alix,' he said, 'the tapping is going on—a little farther off now, and then it comes back again, as if it was to lead us on. It must be on purpose.'

CHAPTER III

THE CARETAKER

'LET'S follow it along,' said Alix, after another moment or two's hesitation.

They were standing, as I said, not many yards from the end of the wall, and thither the sound seemed to lead them. When they got quite to the corner the tapping had stopped. But the children were not discouraged.

'That's what fairies do,' said Alix, as if all her life she had lived on intimate terms with the beings she spoke of. 'They show you a bit, and then they leave you to find out a bit for yourself. We must poke about now and see what we can find.'

Rafe had already set to work in this way : he was feeling and prodding the big, solid-looking stones which finished off the corner.

'Alix,' he exclaimed, 'one of these stones shakes a little ; let's push at it together.'

Yes, there was no doubt that it yielded a little, especially at one side. The children pushed with all their might and main, but for some time an uncertain sort of wobbling was the only result. Rafe stood back a little to recover his breath, and to look at the stone more critically.

'There may be some sort of spring or hinge about it,' he said at last. 'Give me the parasol again, Alix.'

He then pressed the point of it firmly along the side of the stone, down the seam of mortar which appeared to join it to its neighbour in

the wall.   He need not have pressed
so hard, for when he got to the middle
of the line the stone suddenly yielded,
turning inwards so quickly and sharply
that Rafe almost fell forward on the
parasol, and a square dark hole was
open before them.

Alix darted forward and peeped in.

'Rafe,' she cried, 'there's a sort of
handle inside; shall I try to turn it?'

She did so without waiting for his
answer.   It moved quite easily, and
then they found that the two or three
stones completing the row to the
ground, below the one that had already
opened, were really only thin slabs
joined together and forming a little
door.   It was like the doors you sometimes see in a library, which on the
outside have the appearance of a row
of books.

The opening was now clear before
them, and they did not hesitate to pass
through.   They had to stoop a little,
but once within, it was easy to stand

upright, and even side by side. Alix caught hold of Rafe's hand.

'Let's keep fast hold of each other,' she whispered.

For a few steps they advanced in almost total darkness, for the door behind them had noiselessly closed. But this was in the nature of things, and quite according to Alix's programme.

'I only hope,' she went on, 'that we haven't somehow or other got inside the cave where the pied piper took the children. It might have an opening into England somehow, even though I think Hamelin was in Germany; but, of course, there's nothing to be frightened at, is there, Rafe?' though her own heart was beating fast.

Rafe's only answer was a sort of grunt, which expressed doubt, though we will not say fear. Perhaps it was the safest answer he could make under the very peculiar circumstances. But no doubt it was a great relief to both when, before they had time really to ask themselves whether they were frightened or not, a faint light showed itself in front of them, growing stronger and brighter as they stepped on, till at last they could clearly make out in what sort of a place they were.

It was a short, fairly wide passage, seemingly hollowed out of the ground, and built up in the same way as the wall outside into the soil—in fact it was like a small tunnel. The light was of a reddish hue, and soon they saw the reason of this. It came from an inner room, the door of which was half open, where a fire was brightly burning, and by the hearth sat a small figure.

The children looked at each other, then they bent forward to see more. Noiseless though they were, the little person seemed to know they were coming. She lifted her head, and though her face was partly hidden by the hood of the scarlet cloak which covered her almost entirely, they saw that it was that of a very old woman.

'Welcome, my dears,' she said at once. 'I have been looking for you this long time.'

Her voice, though strange—in what way it was strange the children could not have told, for it seemed to come from far away, and yet it seemed to them that they had often heard it before—encouraged them to step forward.

'Good - morning,' Alix began, but then she hesitated. Was it morning, or evening, or night, or what? It was difficult to believe that only a few minutes ago they had been standing outside in the warm sunshine, with the soft spring breeze wafting among the fresh green leaves, and the birds singing overhead. *That* all seemed a dream. 'I beg your pardon,' the little girl began again; 'I don't quite know what I should say, but thank you for speaking so kindly. How did you know we were coming?'

'I heard you,' replied the old woman. 'I heard your little footsteps up to the gateway yesterday, and I knew you'd come again to-day.'

By this time Rafe had found his tongue too.

'Did you send the wren?' he said.

'Never mind about that just now,' she answered. 'I've many a messenger; and what's better still, I've quick eyes, and even quicker ears, for all that I'm so very old. I know what you want of me, and if you're good children you shall not be disappointed. I've been getting ready for you in more ways than one.'

'Do you mean you've got stories to tell us?' exclaimed the children eagerly.

'Of course,' she replied, with a smile. 'I wouldn't be much good if I hadn't stories for you.'

All this time, I must tell you, the

old woman had been busily knitting. Her needles made a little silvery click, but there was nothing fidgeting about this sound; now and then her words seemed to go in a sort of time with it. What she was knitting they could not see.

Alix gave a deep sigh of satisfaction.

'How beautiful!' she said; 'and may we come every day, and may we stay as long as we like, and will you sometimes invite us to tea, perhaps? and——'

'Alix!' said Rafe, in a tone of reproval.

'Nay, nay,' said their hostess. 'Let her chatter. All in good time, my love,' she added to Alix, and the click of the needles seemed to repeat the words, 'All in good time,' like a little song.

Rafe's eyes, which were sometimes more observant than Alix's, as his tongue did not use up so much of his attention as hers, had meanwhile been wandering round the room. It can, I

think, be best described as a very cosy
kitchen, but, unlike many kitchens, it
was fresh and not the least too hot.
There was a strange, pleasant fragrance
in the air that made one think of pine
woods.   Afterwards the children found
out that this came from the fire, for it
was entirely of fir-cones, of which a
large heap stood neatly stacked in one
corner.

A long chain hung down the chimney,
with a hook at the end, to which a
bright red copper pan was fastened;
a little kettle of the same metal stood
on the hearthstone, which was snowy
white.   The walls of the room were of
rough stone, redder in colour than the
wall outside, or else the firelight made
them seem so.   Behind where the old
woman sat hung a grass-green curtain,
closely drawn; there was no lamp or
candle, but the firelight was quite
enough.   A wooden dresser ran along
one side, and on its shelves were ar-
ranged cups and plates and jugs of the

queerest shapes and colours you could imagine. I must tell you more about these later on. There was a settle with a very curious patchwork cushion, but besides this and the rocking-chair on which sat the old woman—I forgot to say that she was sitting on a rocking-chair—the only seats were two little three-legged stools. The middle of the floor was covered by matting of a kind the children had never seen; it was shaded brown, and made you think of a path strewn over with fallen leaves in autumn.

The old woman's kindly tone encouraged Rafe to speak in his turn.

'May I ask you one or two things,' he said, 'before you begin telling us the stories?'

'As many as you like, my boy,' she replied cheerfully. 'I don't say I'll answer them all—that's rather a different matter—but you can ask all the same.'

'It's so puzzling,' said Rafe, hesitating a little. 'I don't think it puzzles Alix so much as me; she knows more about fairy things, I think. I do so want to know if you've lived here a very long time. Have you always lived here—even when the old house was standing and there were people in it?'

'Never mind about always,' replied the old woman. 'A very, very long time? Yes, longer than you could understand, even if I explained it! Long before the old house was pulled down? Yes, indeed, long before the old house was ever thought of! I'm the caretaker here nowadays, you see.'

'The caretaker!' Rafe repeated; 'but there's no house to take care of.'

'There's a great deal to take care of nevertheless,' she replied. 'Think of all the creatures up in the garden, the birds and the butterflies, not to speak of the flowers and the blossom. Ah, yes! we caretakers have a busy time of it, I can tell you, little as you might think it. *And* the stories—why, if I had nothing else to do, the looking after them would keep me busy. They take a deal of tidying. You'd scarcely believe the state they come home in sometimes when they've been out for a ramble—all torn and jagged and draggle-tailed, or else, what's worse, dressed up in such vulgar new clothes that their own mother, and I'm as good as their mother, would scarcely know them again. No, no,' and she shook her head, 'I've no patience with such ways.'

Alix looked delighted. She quite understood the old woman.

'How nicely you say it,' she exclaimed. 'It's like something papa told us the other day about legends; don't you remember, Rafe?'

Rafe's slower wits were still rather perplexed, but he took things comfortably. Somehow he no longer remembered any more questions to ask. The old woman's bright eyes as she looked at him gave him a pleasant, contented feeling.

'Have you got a story quite ready for us?' asked Alix.

'One, two, three, four,' said the old woman, counting her stitches. 'I'm setting it on, my dear; it'll be ready directly. But what have you got in your basket? It's your dinner, isn't it? You must be getting hungry. Wouldn't you like to eat something while the story's getting ready?'

'Are you going to *knit* the story?' said Alix, looking very surprised.

'Oh dear no!' said the old woman, smiling. 'It's only a way I have. The knitting keeps it straight, otherwise it might fly off once I've let it out. Now open your basket and let's see what you've got for your dinner. There, set it on the table, and you may reach down plates and jugs for yourselves.'

'It's nothing much,' said Alix, 'just some sandwiches and two hard-boiled eggs and some slices of cake.'

'Very good things in their way,' said the old woman, as Alix unpacked the little parcels and laid them on the plates which Rafe handed her from the dresser. 'And if you look into my larder you'll find some fruit, maybe, which won't go badly for dessert. What should you say to strawberries and cream?'

She nodded towards one corner of the kitchen where there was a little door which the children had not before noticed, so very neatly was it fitted into the wall.

The opening of it was another surprise; the 'larder' was quite different from the room inside. It was a little arbour, so covered over with greenery that you could not see through the leaves to the outside, though the sunshine managed to creep in here and there, and the twittering of the birds was clearly heard.

On a stone slab stood a curiously-shaped basket filled with—oh! such

lovely strawberries ! and beside it a
bowl of tempting yellow cream ; these
were the only eatables to be seen in
the larder.

'Strawberries !' exclaimed Rafe ;
' just fancy, Alix, and it's only
April.'

'But we're in Fairyland, you stupid
boy,' said Alix ; 'or at least somewhere
very near it.'

'Quick, children,' came the old
woman's voice from the kitchen. 'You
bring the strawberries, Alix, and Rafe
the cream.   There'll be no time for
stories if you dawdle !'

This made them hurry back, and
soon they were seated at the table,
with all the nice things neatly before
them.   They were not greedy children
fortunately, for, as everybody knows,
fairy-folk hold few things in greater
horror than greediness ; and they were
orderly children too.   They packed up
their basket neatly again when they
had finished, and Alix asked if they

should wash up the plates that had been lent to them, which seemed to please their old friend, for she smiled as she replied that it wasn't necessary.

' My china is of a different kind from any you've ever seen,' she said. '*Whiff*, plates,' she added; and then, to the children's amusement, there was a slight rattle, and all the crockery was up in its place again, shining as clean and bright as before it had been used.

There was now no doubt at all that they were really in Fairyland.

CHAPTER IV

THE STORY OF THE THREE WISHES

'AND now for a story,' said Alix joyfully. 'May we sit close beside you, Mrs. —oh dear! Mayn't we call you something?'

'Anything you like,' replied the old woman, smiling.

'I know,' cried Alix; 'Mrs. Caretaker—will that do? It's rather a nice name when you come to think of it.'

'Yes,' agreed their old friend; 'and it should be everybody's name, more or less, if everybody did their duty.

There's no one without something to take care of.'

'No,' said Rafe thoughtfully; 'I suppose not.'

'Draw the two little stools close beside me—one at the right, one at the left; and if you like, you may lean your heads on my knee, you'll hear none the worse.'

'Oh, that's beautiful,' said Alix; 'it's like the children and the white lady. Do you know about the white lady?' she went on, starting up suddenly.

Mrs. Caretaker nodded.

'Oh yes,' she said; 'she's a relation of mine. But we mustn't chatter any more if you're to have a story.'

And the children sat quite silent.

Click, click, went the knitting-needles.

THE STORY OF THE THREE WISHES

That was the name of the first of Mrs. Caretaker's stories.

Once upon a time there lived two sisters in a cottage on the edge of a forest. It was rather a lonely place in some ways, though there was an old town not more than a mile off, where there were plenty of friendly people. But it was lonely in this way, that but seldom any of the townsfolk passed near the cottage, or cared to come to see the sisters, even though they were good and pretty girls, much esteemed by all who knew them.

For the forest had a bad name. Nobody seemed to know exactly why, or what the bad name meant, but there it was. Even in the bright long summer days the children of the town would walk twice as far on the other side to gather posies of the pretty wood-flowers in a little copse, not to be compared with the forest for beauty, rather than venture within its shade. And the young men and maidens of a summer evening, though occasionally they might come to its outskirts in their strolls, were never tempted to do more than stand for a moment or two glancing along its leafy glades. Only the sisters, Arminel and Chloe, had sometimes entered the forest, though but for a little way, and not without some fear and trembling.

But they had no misgiving as to living in its near neighbourhood. Custom does a great deal, and here in the cottage by the forest-side they had spent all their lives. And the grandmother, who had taken care of them since they had been left orphans in their babyhood, told them there was no need for fear so long as they loved each other and did their duty. All the same, she never denied that the great forest was an uncanny place.

This was the story of it, so far as any one knew. Long, long ago, when many things in the world were different from what they are now, a race of giants, powerful and strong, were the owners of the forest, and so long as

they were just and kindly · to their
weaker neighbours, all went well. But
after a while they grew proud and
tyrannical, and did some very cruel
things. Then their power was taken
from them, and they became, as a
punishment, as weak and puny as they
had been the opposite. Now and
then, so it was said about the country-
side, one or two of them had been
seen, miserable-looking little dwarfs.
And the seeing of them was the great
thing to be dreaded, for it was supposed
to be a certain sign of bad luck.

But the grandmother had heard
more than this, though where, or when,
or how, she could not remember. The
spell over the forest dwarfs was not to
be for ever; something some day was to
break it, though what she did not know.

'And who can tell,' she would say
now and then, 'how better things may
come about for the poor creatures?
There's maybe a reason for your being
here, children. Keep love and pity in

your hearts, and never let any fear
prevent you doing a kind action if it
comes in your way.'

But till now, though they had gone
on living in the old cottage since their
grandmother's death in the same way,
never forgetting what she had said,
Arminel and Chloe had never caught
sight of their strange neighbours. True,
once or twice they had seen a small
figure scuttering away when they had
ventured rather farther than usual along
the forest paths, but then it might have
been only some wild wood creature, of
whom, no doubt, there were many who
had their dwellings in the lonely gloom.
Sometimes a strange curiosity really to
see one of the dwarfs for themselves
would come over them ; they often
talked about it in the long winter
evenings when they had nothing to
amuse them.

But it was only to each other that
they talked in this way. To their
friends in the town, for they had friends

there whom they saw once a week on the market-day, they never chattered about the forest or the dwarfs; and when they were asked why they went on living in this strange and lonely place, they smiled and said it was their home, and they were happier there than anywhere else.

And so they were. They were very busy to begin with, for their butter and eggs and poultry were more prized than any to be had far or near. Arminel was the dairy-woman, and Chloe the hen-wife, and at the end of each week they would count up their earnings, eager to see which had made the more by their labours. Fortunately for their happy feelings to each other, up till now their gains had been pretty nearly equal, for there is no saying where jealousy will not creep in, even between the dearest of friends.

But quite lately, for the first time, things had not been going so well. It was late in the autumn, and there had

been unusually heavy rains, and when
they ceased the winter seemed to begin
all at once, and before its time, and the
animals suffered for it. The cow's milk
fell off before Arminel had looked for
its doing so, and some great plans
which she had been making for the
future seemed likely to be disappointed.
She had hoped to save enough through
the winter to buy another cow in the
spring, so that with the two she would
have had a supply of butter for her
customers in the town all the year
round. And Chloe's hens were not
doing well either. One or two of them
had even died, and she couldn't get her
autumn chickens to fatten. Worst of
all, the eggs grew fewer day by day.

These misfortunes distressed the
sisters very much. Sadder still, they
grew irritable and short-tempered, each
reproaching the other, and making out
that she herself had managed better.

'It is all your want of foresight,' said
Arminel to Chloe one market-day when

the egg-basket looked but poorly filled. 'Everybody knows that hens stop laying with the first cold. You should have potted some eggs a few weeks ago when they were so plentiful.'

'My customers don't care for potted eggs,' said Chloe. 'Till now I have always had a pretty fair supply of fresh ones, except for a week or two about Christmas time. How should I have known that this year would be different from other years? If you are so wonderfully wise, why did you not bring Strawberry indoors a month sooner than usual? It is evident that she has caught cold. You need not sneer at my eggs when you count your pats of butter. Why, there are not above half what you had two months ago.'

'When you manage your own affairs properly, you may find fault with mine,' said Arminel snappishly.

And they felt so unamiable towards each other that all the way to market and back they walked on separate sides of the road without speaking a word.

Such a state of things had never been known before.

It was late when they got home that afternoon, and being a dull and cloudy day it was almost dark. The poor girls felt tired and unhappy, for each was sad with the double sadness of having to bear her troubles alone. And besides this, there is nothing more tiring than ill-temper.

Arminel sat down weariedly on a chair. The fire was out; the cottage felt very chilly; the one little candle which Chloe had lighted gave but a feeble ray. Arminel sighed deeply. Chloe, whose heart was very soft, felt sorry for her, and setting down her basket began to see to the fire.

'Leave it alone,' said her sister. 'We may as well go to bed without any supper. I'm too tired to eat; and it's just as well to get accustomed to scanty fare. It is what is before us, I suppose.'

'You need not be quite so down-hearted,' said Chloe, persevering in her efforts. 'Things may mend again. I sold my eggs for more than ever before. It seems that everybody's hens are doing badly. I'll have the fire burning in a minute, and some nice hot coffee ready, and then you'll feel better.'

But Arminel was not to be so easily consoled.

'If you've done well with your eggs it's more than I did with my butter,' she said. 'Dame Margery, the house-keeper from the castle, says she'll take no more from me if I can't promise as much as last year. She doesn't like to go changing about for her butter, she says; and mine was enough for the ladies.'

'I'm sure you've enough for two ladies still,' said Chloe.

'Yes; but if I don't keep a little for my other customers, they won't come back to me when I have plenty again,' answered her sister, who seemed deter-

mined to look on the black side of
things.

Then, unluckily, in spite of Chloe's
care, the cold and the damp of the
chimney made the fire smoke ; great
clouds puffed out, almost filling the
kitchen.

' I wish you had let me go to bed,'
said Arminel hastily ; and Chloe's
patience being exhausted, she retorted
by calling her sister unkind and un-
grateful.

The smoke was very disagreeable,
no doubt. Arminel opened the window
wide to let it clear off. The wind was
blowing from the forest which lay on
this side of the house. All looked
dark and gloomy, and Arminel gave a
little shiver as she glanced out. Suddenly she started.

' Chloe,' she said, ' did you hear
that ? '

' What ? ' said Chloe.

' A cry—yes, there it is again, as if
some one was in great trouble.'

Chloe heard it too, but she was feeling rather sulky and contradictory.

'It's nothing,' she said. 'Only a hare or some wild creature; they often scream,' and she turned back to the table where she was preparing coffee.

But though the room was now pretty clear of smoke and the fire was behaving better, Arminel did not close the window. She still stood by it listening. And again there came the strange shrill yet feeble cry, telling unmistakably of anguish, or whether of beast or man no one could have told. And this time Chloe stood still with the kettle in her hand, more startled than she had been before.

'Sister,' said Arminel decidedly, 'that is not the squeal of a hare; it is something worse. Perhaps some child from the town may have strayed into the forest and got benighted. It is possible at least. And the forest is not like other places. Who knows what might happen to one astray there?'

'What could we do in such a case?' said Chloe. 'We're not all-powerful.'

She spoke more out of a little remaining temper than from cowardice or indifference, for like her sister she was both brave and kind.

'Remember what our grandmother said,' said Arminel, and she repeated the grandmother's words: '"Never hang back from doing a kind action; no harm can come to you while you love each other and do your duty." I am going alone to the forest if you will not come,' she went on, and she turned towards the door as she spoke.

'Of course I will come with you,' said Chloe, reaching down her mantle and hood which she had hung up on a nail. 'Close the window, Arminel,' she said. 'I'll leave the coffee on the hob. The fire is burning nicely now, and we shall find it bright and warm when we come back.'

As they stepped outside, closing the door behind them, the cry broke out

again.   Tired though they were with
their long day at market, the sisters
set off running.   Two or three fields
lay between them and the edge of the
wood, and part of the way the ground
was very rough, but they were nimble
and sure-footed.   And ever as they ran
came the cries, feebler yet more distinct, and before long they could distinguish the words, 'Help! comrades,
help!'

'It is not a hare, you see,' said
Arminel.

'No, indeed,' answered Chloe, and
both felt a thrill of fear, though they
only ran the faster.

The cries, though now they grew
rarer, becoming indeed mingled with
groans, still served to guide them.
Soon they were in the midst of the
trees, making their way more by a
sort of instinct, for it was almost dark.
Suddenly a ray of moonlight glimmered
through the firs, and a few paces in
front of them they saw lying on the

ground a small dark object writhing and groaning.

Just here the trees were not so thick. It was like a little clearing. The girls stepped onwards cautiously, catching hold of each other.

'It is—'whispered Arminel—'Oh, Chloe, it is one of the dwarfs.'

'Courage,' murmured Chloe in return, though her own heart was beating very fast. 'He seems in no state to hurt us now, if only it be not a trick.'

The groans had ceased, and when they got close to the strange figure on the ground it seemed quite motionless. The moonlight had grown stronger. They stooped down and examined the dwarf. His eyes were closed; his face was wrinkled and brown; he was brown all over. He wore a furry coat, much the same colour as his own skin.

Arminel lifted one of his queer claw-like hands; it fell down again by his side.

'I believe he is dead,' she said. 'I didn't know the dwarfs ever could die. What shall we do, Chloe? We cannot leave him here, in case he should be still living.'

'We must carry him home, I'm afraid,' said Chloe. 'Yes, I'm afraid we must, for see, Arminel, he's opening his eyes,' as two bright black beads suddenly glanced up at them.

'Nimbo, Hugo,' said a weak, hoarse little voice. 'Are you there? No,' and the dwarf opened his eyes more widely, and tried to sit up. 'No,' he went on, 'it is not my comrades! Who are you?' and he shuddered as if with fear.

CHAPTER V

THE STORY OF THE THREE WISHES
(*continued*)

T was indeed a turning of the tables for a dwarf to be afraid of them. It gave the sisters courage to speak to him.

'We heard your cries,' said Arminel. 'Ever so far off in our cottage across the fields we heard them. What is the matter? Have you hurt yourself?'

The little man groaned.

'I have had a fall,' he said, 'from a branch of the tree under which I am lying. I climbed up to shake down some large fir-cones, and lost my

footing.   I have hurt myself sadly.   I
feel bruised all over.   How I shall
ever get back to my comrades I do
not know,' and again he groaned.

He was not a very courageous dwarf
evidently ; perhaps the courage of the
race had been lost with its stature !
But the sisters felt very sorry for him.

' Have you broken any bones, do you
think?' said Chloe, who was very practical.

The dwarf turned and twisted himself about with many sighs and moans.

'No,' said he, 'I think I am only
bruised and terribly cold.   I have been
lying here so long, so long.   I cannot
go home ; they are miles away in the
centre of the forest.'

Arminel and Chloe considered.   They
did not much like the idea of the uncanny creature spending a night under
their roof, even though they no longer
feared that he was playing them any
trick.   If the mere sight of a dwarf
brought ill-luck, what might not they
expect from the visit of one of the

spell-bound race? But their grandmother's words returned to their mind.

'You must come home with us,' they
said, speaking together. 'We can at
least give you shelter and warmth, and
a night's rest may do you much good.'

'There is the salve for bruises which
granny taught us to make,' added Chloe.
'We have some of it by us, I know.'

The dwarf gave a sigh of relief.

'Maidens,' he said, 'you shall never
have cause to regret your kindness. I
know your cottage. We have often
watched you when you little knew it.
I think I could make shift to walk
there if you will each give me an arm.'

They got him to his feet with some
difficulty. He was so small, hardly
reaching up to their elbows, that it
ended in their almost carrying him
between them. And they seemed to
get home much more quickly than
they had come, even though they
walked slowly. The dwarf knew every
step of the way, and his queer bead-

F

like eyes pierced through the darkness as if it had been noonday.

'A little to the right,' he would say,
or, 'a few paces to the left, the ground
is better.'

And almost before they knew where
they were they found themselves before
their own door. The wind had gone
down, all was peaceful and still, and
inside the kitchen was a picture of
comfort, the fire burning red and
cheerily.

'Ah,' said the little man, when they
had settled him on a stool in front of
the hearth, 'this is good!' and he
stretched out his small brown hands
to the ruddy glow. 'It is long since
I have seen such a fire, and very long
since I have been in a room like this.'

But then he grew quite silent, and
the sisters did not like to ask him
what he meant.

Chloe busied herself with the coffee
which boiled up in no time; and in
the larder, to her surprise, when she

went in to fetch a loaf of bread intended for the sisters' supper, she
found a pat of butter and a jug of
cream which she had not known were
there. She was very pleased, for both
she and Arminel had hospitable hearts,
and she would have been sorry to have
had nothing for their guest but dry
bread and skim-milk coffee.

'Arminel,' she said, as she came
back into the kitchen, 'you had forgotten this cream and butter, fortunately so, for now we can give our
friend a nice supper.'

Arminel looked quite astonished.

'I took all the butter there was with
me to market this morning, and I
never keep cream except for our Sun-
day treat.'

But there was another surprise in
store.

Arminel in her turn went into the
larder.

'Chloe!' she called out, 'see what
you have forgotten. Eggs!' and she

held up three large, beautiful brown
eggs.

'I don't know where they have
come from,' said Chloe. 'I'm certain
they were not there when I packed
my basket. Besides, none of my hens
lay eggs of that colour.'

'Never mind,' said the dwarf; 'here
they are, and that is enough. We
shall now have an omelette for supper.
An omelette and hot coffee! That is a
supper for a king.'

He seemed to be getting quite
bright and cheerful, and complained
no more of his bruises as he sat there
basking in the pleasant warmth of the
fire. Supper was soon ready, and the
three spent a pleasant evening; the
little man asking the sisters many
questions about their life and occupa-
tions. They told him all about
their present troubles, and he told
them to keep up heart, and never
forget their good grandmother's
counsel.

'Did you know our grandmother?'
they asked in surprise.

'I have heard of her,' was all he
said; and though they were curious
to know more, they did not venture
to question him further.

After supper they made up a bed
for him on the kitchen settle, where
he said he was sure he would sleep
most comfortably.

'And now farewell,' he added; 'I
shall be off in the morning before you
are stirring. Your kindness has so
refreshed me that I feel sure I shall
be able to make my way home without
difficulty.'

He gave a little sigh as he spoke.

'I would fain do what I can in
return for your goodness,' he continued. 'Some things are still in my
power. I can give you three wishes
which, under certain conditions, will
be fulfilled.'

The sisters' eyes sparkled with delight.

'Oh, thank you a thousand times,' they said. 'Pray tell us what we must do, and we will follow your orders exactly.'

'Three wishes between you are all I can give,' he replied. 'One each, and the fulfilment of these depends upon the third, to which a secret is attached, and this secret you must discover for yourselves. The key of it is, I trust, in your own hearts.'

'We will do our best to find it,' said Arminel. 'If it has to do with our love for each other you may trust us. Chloe and I never quarrel.'

But suddenly, as she said this, the remembrance of that day struck her, and she grew red, feeling the dwarf's eyes fixed upon her.

'At least,' she added hurriedly, 'I should say we seldom quarrel, though I'm afraid our anxieties lately have not sweetened our tempers.'

'Beware, then, for the future,' said the dwarf. 'All will depend on yourselves.'

The sisters went to bed full of
eagerness and hopefulness, longing for
the next day to come that they might
decide how to use their strange friend's
gift.

'I shall not be able to sleep,' said
Arminel; 'my head is so full of the
three wishes.'

'And so is mine,' said her sister.
'You shall have the first, Arminel, and
I the second. The third will be the
one to ponder over.'

'I shall have no difficulty in de-
ciding,' said Arminel. 'And you,
Chloe, being the younger, must, of
course, be guided partly by my
advice.'

'I don't see that at all,' said Chloe.
'The dwarf said nothing about elder
or younger, and———'

At this moment a loud snore from
the kitchen reminded them that their
guest was still there.

'Dear, dear,' said Chloe. 'What
would he think if he heard us begin-

ning to quarrel already? We must beware.'

But Arminel was not so ready to give in, and there is no saying what might not have befallen, had it not happened that the moment her head touched the pillow she fell fast asleep. And Chloe quickly followed her example.

They awoke later than usual the next morning, feeling quite rested and refreshed.

'I never slept so soundly in my life,' said Arminel. 'I suppose it was with being so tired.'

'I don't know,' said Chloe. 'I have an idea that our friend had something to do with our falling asleep so quickly to prevent us quarrelling. Now, Arminel, whatever we do, let us remember his warning.'

'Of course, I don't want to quarrel,' her sister replied. 'We didn't need the dwarf to come here to tell us to be good friends. But, after all, his promise

of fulfilling our wishes may be nonsense.
I long to test it.   I wonder if he is still
there, by the bye.'

No, he was gone ; the little bed they
had made up for him on the settle, of
some extra blankets and pillows, was
neatly folded away.   The fire was
already lighted and burning brightly,
the kettle singing on the hearth—the
room showed signs of having been
carefully swept and dusted, and the
window was slightly open to admit a
breath of the fresh morning air.

'Good little dwarf!' exclaimed Arminel.   'I wish he would pay us a visit
often if he helps us so nicely with our
work.'

They sat down to breakfast in the
best of spirits ; and when the meal was
over, and they went out, they found
that the dwarf's good offices had not
been confined to the house.   The
cow was carefully foddered, and looking
most prosperous and comfortable—the
poultry had been seen to, the hen-

house cleaned out, and already, early as it was, several lovely cream white eggs had been laid in the nests.

All this was very encouraging.

'There can be no sort of doubt,' said Chloe, 'that our friend, dwarf though he be, has a kind heart and magic power. I feel certain his promises are to be relied upon. But remember, Arminel, the first two wishes will be no good unless we agree about the third. What shall we do?'

'I propose,' said Arminel, who had plenty of good sense, 'that we go about our work as usual till this evening. Then each of us will have had time to decide as to her own wish, and each of us can propose something for the third. As to the third, we can then consult together.'

To this Chloe agreed.

They spoke little to each other during the day, but when the light began to fail their work was over. They sat down together by the fire.

'Now for a good talk,' said Chloe.
'We have the whole evening before
us.'

'Five minutes would be enough for
me,' said Arminel. 'I've got my wish
cut and dry. I have been longing to
tell you all day, but I thought it best
to keep to our determination of this
morning.'

'How strange!' said Chloe. 'I am
just in the same condition. I decided
upon my wish almost immediately.
Tell me what yours is, and I will tell
you mine.'

'My wish,' said Arminel, 'is to have
a cow. A dun-coloured cow I think
I should prefer—I can picture her so
sweet and pretty—who would give
milk all the year round without ever
running short.'

'Excellent,' cried Chloe; 'my wish
goes well with yours. For what I
want is a dozen hens who would each
lay an egg every morning in the year
without fail. I should thus have as

many fresh eggs as I could possibly want, and enough to spare for setting whenever I liked. Some of my present hens are very good mothers, and would hatch them beautifully.'

'I think your wish a very good one,' said Arminel. 'But now as to the fulfilment. We have now expressed our wishes distinctly, but there is no use as yet in going to look for the new cow in the shed or hens in the hen-house, seeing that there remains, alas! the third one! What can it be?'

'Could it be for a hen-house?' said Chloe; 'my poor hens are not very well off in their present one, and it is right to make one's animals comfortable; so this would be a kind-hearted wish.'

'Not more than to wish for a warm shed for my cows,' said Arminel. 'Cows require much more care than hens. I daresay that is what we are meant to wish for.'

'I am certain it is not,' said Chloe.

' At least, if you wish for a cow-shed, *I* wish for a hen-house.'

'That, of course, is nonsense,' said Arminel. 'I feel sure the dwarf meant we were to agree in what we wished for. And if you were amiable and unselfish you would join with me, Chloe.'

'I might say precisely the same thing to you,' said Chloe coldly.

And though they went on talking till bed-time they came to no conclusion. Indeed, I fear a good many sharp and unkind words passed between them, and they went to bed without saying good-night to each other. So far it did not seem as if the dwarf's gift was to bring them happiness.

CHAPTER VI

THE STORY OF THE THREE WISHES
(*concluded*)

HEN they woke in the morn-
ing they were in a calmer
state of mind, and began
to see how foolish they
had been.

'Chloe,' said Arminel, as they sat
at breakfast, 'we were very nearly
quarrelling last night ; and if we quarrel
we shall certainly never find out the
secret of the third wish ; and all our
hopes will be at an end. Now, let us
think over quietly what the third wish
is likely to be. Let me see—what
were the dwarf's exact words ? '

'He said we must seek for it in our own hearts,' replied Chloe. 'That means, of course, that it must be something kind.'

'Perhaps he meant that it must be something to do us both good,' said Arminel. 'What is there we are equally in want of? Oh! I know; suppose we wish for a good stack of fuel for the winter. That would certainly benefit us both."

'It can do no harm to try,' said Chloe; 'so I agree to the wish for a stack of fuel.'

Arminel's eyes sparkled.

'I daresay we have guessed it,' she exclaimed, jumping up. 'Come out at once to see, Chloe.'

But, alas! the heap of brushwood for their winter's firing, in the corner of the yard, had grown no bigger than the day before. No fresh sounds of cheerful cackling reached them from the hen-house; and Strawberry stood alone in her stall.

The wishes were still unfulfilled.

The sisters returned to the house rather crestfallen.

'What can it be?' said Arminel; and this time Chloe made a suggestion.

'Supposing we wish that the copper coins we have put aside for our Christmas charities should be turned into silver,' she said. 'That would be a kind thought for the very poor folk we try to help a little.'

'As you like,' said her sister; 'but I doubt its being any use. We are always told that charity which costs us nothing is little worth.'

She was right. When they opened the little box which held the coins she spoke of, there they still were, copper as before, so this time it was no use to look outside for the new cow and hens. And all through the day they went on thinking first of one thing, then of another, without any success, so that by the evening their work had suffered from their neglect, and they went tired and dispirited to bed.

The next day they were obliged to work doubly hard to make up, and one or two new ideas occurred to them which they put to the test, always, alas ! with the same result.

' We are wasting our time and our temper for no use,' said Arminel at last. ' I am afraid the truth is that the dwarf was only playing us a mischievous trick.' And even Chloe was forced to allow that it seemed as if her sister was in the right.

' We will try to forget all about it,' said Arminel. ' It must be indeed true that having anything to do with the dwarfs only brings bad luck.'

But though she spoke courageously, Chloe was wakened in the night by hearing her sister crying softly to her-self.

' Poor dear Arminel,' thought Chloe, though she took care to lie quite still as if sleeping. ' I do feel for her. If I

had but my hens I could soon make
up to her for her disappointment.'

But of course as the dun cow did
not come, neither did the fairy hens,
and a time of really great anxiety
began for the sisters. Strawberry's milk
dwindled daily ; so did the number of
eggs, till at last something very like real
poverty lay before them. They were
almost ashamed to go to market, so
little had they to offer to their customers. Never had they been so unhappy or distressed.

But out of trouble often comes good.
Their affection for each other grew
stronger, and all feelings of jealousy died
away as each felt more and more sorry
for her sister.

'If only we had never gone near the
wood,' said Arminel one evening when
things were looking very gloomy indeed,
'none of these worst troubles would
have come upon us, I feel sure. I begin
to believe everything that has been said
about those miserable dwarfs. It is

very good of you, dear Chloe, not to blame me as the cause of all our misfortunes, for it was I who heard the cries in the wood and made you come with me to see what was the matter.'

'How could I blame you?' said Chloe. 'We did it together, and it was what grandmother would have wished. If we had not gone we should always have reproached ourselves for not doing a kind action, and even as things are, even supposing we are suffering from the dwarf's spitefulness, it is better to suffer with a clear conscience than to prosper with a bad one.'

Her words comforted her sister a little. They kissed each other affectionately and went to bed, sad at heart certainly, but not altogether despondent.

In the night Arminel awoke. There was bright moonlight in the room, and as she glanced at her sleeping sister, she saw traces of tears on Chloe's pale face.

'My poor sister!' she said to her-self. 'She has been crying, and would not let me know it. I do not care for myself, if only dear Chloe could have her hens. I could bear the disap-pointment about my cow. How I wish it might be so.'

As the thought passed through her mind, a sweet feeling of peace and satisfaction stole over her. She closed her eyes and almost immediately fell asleep, and slept soundly.

Very soon after this in her turn Chloe awoke. She, too, sat up and looked at her sister. There was a smile on Arminel's sleeping face which touched Chloe almost more than the traces of tears on her own had touched her sister.

'Poor dear Arminel,' she thought. 'She is dreaming, perhaps, of her dun cow. How little I should mind my own disappointment if I could see her happy. Oh! I do wish she could have her cow!'

And having thought this, she, too, as her sister had done, fell asleep with a feeling of peace and hopefulness such as she had not had for long.

The winter sun was already some little way up on his journey when the sisters awoke the next morning, for they had slept much later than usual. Arminel was the first to start up with a feeling that something pleasant had happened.

'Chloe!' she exclaimed. 'We have overslept ourselves. And on such a bright morning, too! How can it have happened?'

Chloe opened her eyes and looked about her with a smile.

'Yes, indeed,' she replied. 'One could imagine it was summer time, and I have had such a good night, and such pleasant dreams.'

'So have I,' answered her sister. 'And I am so hungry!'

That was scarcely to be wondered at, for they had gone almost supperless to bed, and there was little if anything in the larder for their breakfast.

'I am hungry too,' said Chloe. 'But I am afraid there isn't much for our breakfast. However, I feel in much better spirits, though I don't know why.'

Chloe was ready a little before her sister, and hastened into the kitchen, to light the fire and prepare such food as there was. But just as Arminel was turning to follow her, she was startled by a cry from Chloe.

'Sister!' she called. 'Come quick! See what I have found!'

She was in the larder, which served them also as a dairy. Arminel hurried in. There stood Chloe, her face rosy with pleasure and surprise, a basket in her hands full of beautiful large eggs of the same rich browny colour as those which had come so mysteriously the evening of the dwarf's visit.

'After all,' said Chloe, 'I believe the little man meant well by us. It

must be he who has sent these eggs.
Oh, Arminel! do let us try again
to discover the secret of the third
wish!'

But Arminel didn't seem to hear
what her sister was saying. Her eyes
were fixed in amazement on the stone
slab behind where Chloe was standing.
There were two large bowls filled to
the brim with new milk; it was many
weeks since such a sight had been seen
in the cottage.

'Chloe,' was all she could say as she
pointed it out to her sister.

Chloe did not speak; she darted
outside closely followed by Arminel.
The same idea had come to them both,
and they were not mistaken in it. There
in the cow-house, in the hitherto un-
used stall beside Strawberry's, stood the
dearest little cow you could picture to
yourself, dun-coloured, sleek, and silky,
as if indeed she had just come from
fairyland. She turned her large soft
brown eyes on Arminel as the happy

girl ran up to her, and gave a low soft
'moo,' as if to say—'You're my dear
mistress. I know you will be kind to
me, and in return I promise you that
you shall find me the best of cows.'

But Arminel only waited to give her
one loving pat, and then hurried off to
the poultry yard.

There too a welcome sight awaited
them. Twelve beautiful white hens
were pecking about, and as Chloë drew
near them she was greeted with clucks
of welcome as the pretty creatures ran
towards her.

'They know they belong to you,
Chloe, you see,' said Arminel. 'They
are asking for their breakfast! See,
what is that sack in the corner? it looks
like corn for them.'

So it was, and in another moment
Chloe had thrown them out a good
handful, in which her old hens were
allowed to share. Poor things, they had
not had too much to eat just lately, and
evidently the new-comers were of most

amiable dispositions. 'All promised peace and prosperity.

The sisters made their way back to their little kitchen, but though they had now eggs in plenty and new milk for their coffee they felt too excited to eat.

'How can it have come about?' said Arminel. 'Chloe, have you wished for anything without telling me?'

'Have you?' said Chloe, in her turn. 'One of us wishing alone would not have been enough. All I know is, that in the night I felt so sorry for you that I said to myself if only *your* wish could be fulfilled I would give up my own.'

'How strange!' exclaimed Arminel; 'the very same thing happened to me. I woke up and saw traces of tears on your face, and the thought went through me that if *your* wish could come to pass, I should be content.'

'Then we have found the secret,' said Chloe. 'Each of us was to forget herself for the sake of the other; and the dwarf has indeed been a good friend.'

It would be difficult to describe the happiness that now reigned in the cottage, or the pride with which the sisters set off to market the next time with their well-filled baskets. And all through the winter it was the same. Never did the little cow's milk fail, nor the number of eggs fall off, so that the sisters became quite famous in the neighbourhood for always having a supply of butter, poultry, and eggs of the best quality.

One evening, when the spring time had come round again, the sisters were strolling in the outskirts of the forest, everything was looking calm and peaceful—the ground covered with the early wood-flowers, the little birds twittering softly before they settled to roost for the night.

'How sweet it is here,' said Arminel. 'I never feel now as if I could be the least afraid of the forest, nor of a whole army of dwarfs if we met them.'

'I wish we could meet our dwarf,' said Chloe. 'I would love to thank him for all the happiness he has given us.'

This was a wish they had often expressed before.

'Somehow,' said Arminel, 'I have an idea that the dwarfs no longer inhabit the forest. Everything seems so much brighter and less gloomy than it used to do here. Besides, if our friend were still anywhere near, I cannot help thinking we should have seen him.'

As she said the words, they heard a rustling beside them. Where they stood there was a good deal of undergrowth, and for a moment or two they saw nothing, though the sound continued. Then suddenly a little figure

emerged from among the trees and
stood before them. It was their friend
the dwarf.

At first sight he looked much the
same as when they had last seen him ;
but the moment he began to speak
they felt there was a difference. His
voice was soft and mellow, instead of
harsh and croaking ; his brown eyes
had lost the hunted, suspicious look
which had helped to give him such a
miserable expression.

'I am pleased that you have wished
to see me again,' he said, kindly.

'Oh yes, indeed !' the sisters exclaimed ; 'we can never thank you
enough for the happiness you have
given us.'

'You have yourselves to thank for
it as much as me, my children,' said
the little man ; 'and in discovering
the secret which has brought you
prosperity, you have done for others
also what you had no idea of. The
spell under which I and my comrades

have suffered so long is broken, now
that one of us has been able to be
of real and lasting benefit to some
beings of the race who, ages ago, were
the victims of our cruelty. We are
now leaving the forest for ever. No
longer need the young men and
maidens shrink from strolling under
these ancient trees, or the little children start away in terror from every
rustle among the leaves for fear of
seeing one of us.'

'Are you going to be giants again?'
said Arminel, curiously.

The dwarf smiled.

'That I cannot tell you,' he said, as
he shook his head; 'and what does it
matter? In some far-off land we shall
again be happy, for we shall have learnt
our lesson.'

And before the sisters had time to
speak, he had disappeared; only the
same little rustle among the bushes
was to be heard for a moment or two.
Then all was silent, till a faint 'tu-

whit' from an owl waking up in the distance, and the first glimmer of the moonlight among the branches, warned Arminel and Chloe that it was time for them to be turning homewards.

CHAPTER VII

THE SUMMER PRINCESS

LL was silent too in the little kitchen as the old woman's voice died away and the click of her knitting needles ceased.

Alix was the first to speak.

'That was a lovely story,' she said approvingly. 'It will give Rafe and me a lot to talk about. It is so interesting to think what we would wish for if we had the chance.'

'I'm afraid you mustn't stay with me any longer to talk about it to-day,' said the old woman. 'It is quite—

time—for you—to go home;' and somehow her voice seemed to grow into a sort of singing, and the needles began to click again, though very faintly, as if heard from some way off.

What was the matter?

Alix felt as if she were going to sleep. She rubbed her eyes, but Rafe's voice speaking to her quite clearly and distinctly woke her up again.

'Alix,' he was saying, 'don't you see where we are?' and glancing up, she found that she and her brother were sitting on a moss-grown stone in the old garden, not very far from the gate by which the wren had invited them to enter.

It was growing towards evening. Already the 'going to bed' feeling seemed about in the air. The birds' voices came softly; a little chill evening breeze made the children shiver slightly, though it only meant to wish them 'good-night.'

'It feels like the end of the story,' said Alix. 'Let's go home, Rafe.'

.   .   .   .   .   .

This was how the next story came to be told.

The days had passed happily for Rafe and Alix; the weather had been very fine and mild, and they had played a great deal in the old garden, which grew lovelier every day.

'I hardly feel as if we had anything to wish for just now,' said Alix, one afternoon, when, tired with playing, she and her brother were resting for a little while on the remains of a rustic bench which they had found in a corner under the trees. 'We've been so happy lately, Rafe; haven't we? Ever since that day!'

Somehow they had not talked very much to each other of their visit to the old caretaker; but now and then they had amused themselves by planning what they would have wished for had

H

they come across a dwarf with magic power.

Rafe did not answer for a moment. He was looking up, high up among the branches.

'Hush,' he said, in a half whisper. 'Do you hear that bird, Alix? I never heard a note like it before.'

'Two notes,' said Alix, in the same low voice. 'It's two birds talking to each other, I feel certain.'

'It does sound like it,' said Rafe. 'Oh, I say, Alix, wouldn't you like to understand what they're saying?'

'Yes,' said his sister. 'I do wish we could. There must be some sense in it. It sounds so real and——Look, Rafe,' she went on, 'they're coming nearer us;' and so they were. Still chirping, the birds flew downwards till they lighted on a branch not very far above the children's heads.

Suddenly Alix caught hold of Rafe's arm.

'Be quite, quite still,' she whispered.

'I have an idea that if we listen very carefully we can make sense of what they're saying.'

She almost held her breath, so eager was she; and Rafe, too, sat perfectly motionless. And Alix was not mistaken. After a while the birds' chirps took shape to the children's ears. Bit by bit the 'tweet, tweet' varied and changed, like a voice heard in the distance, which, as it draws nearer, grows from a murmur into syllables and words.

One bird was answering the other; in fact, there was a lively discussion going on between them.

'No, no,' said the first. 'I tell you it is my turn to begin, brother. I have my story quite ready, just as I heard it down there in the sunny lands from one of my companions, and I must tell it at once before I forget it.'

'Mine is ready too,' replied the other bird. 'At least almost. I have just to—think over a few little points, and I am just as anxious as you to amuse the dear children. However, it would be setting them a bad example if we began to quarrel about it, so I will give in. I will fly to a higher branch to meditate a little undisturbed, while you can hop lower still and attract their attention.'

Alix and Rafe looked at each other with a smile as the little fellow fluttered downwards and alighted on a branch still nearer them. There he flapped his wings and cleared his throat.

'Cheep, cheep,' he began. At least that is what it would have sounded to any one else, but the children knew it meant 'good-afternoon.'

'Thank you,' they said. That was not exactly a reply to 'good-afternoon,' certainly; but they meant to thank him for his kind intentions.

'Oh, so you know all about it, I see,' said the bird. 'If you do not mind, I should prefer your making no further observations. It interrupts the thread of my narration.'

The children were perfectly silent. One has to be very careful, you see, when a bird is telling a story; you can't catch hold of him and push him back into the arm-chair, as if he was a big person to be coaxed into entertaining you.

'The title of my story,' began the bird, 'is

'THE SUMMER PRINCESS,'

and again he cleared his throat.

Once upon a time, in a country far to the north of the world, lived a King and a Queen, who had everything they could wish for except an heir to their throne. When I say they had everything they could wish for, that does not mean they had no troubles at all. The Queen thought she had a good many; and the King had one which was more real than any of her fancied ones. He had a wife who was a terrible grumbler. She was a grumbler by nature, and besides this she had been a spoilt child.

As she was very beautiful and could be very sweet and charming when in a contented mood, the King had fallen deeply in love with her when he was on his travels round the world, and had persuaded her to leave her own home in the sunny south to accompany him to his northern kingdom. There she had much to make her happy. Her husband was devoted to her, and while the first bright summer lasted, she almost forgot to grumble, but when the winter came, fierce and boisterous as it always is in those lands, she grew very miserable. She shivered with the cold and instead of bracing herself to bear it, she wrapped herself in her furs and sat from morning till night cowering over a huge fire. In vain the King endeavoured to persuade her to go out with him in his beautiful sledge drawn by the fleetest reindeer, or to make one in the merry skating parties which were the great amusement of his court.

'No, no,' she cried fretfully. 'It would kill me to do anything of the kind.' And though she brightened up as each summer came round, with the return of each winter it was again the same sad story.

As the years passed on another and more real trouble came upon the discontented young Queen. She had no children. She longed so grievously to have a little baby that sometimes she almost forgot her other causes for complaint and left off looking out for the signs of the winter's approach in the melancholy way she was wont to do. So that one day late in the autumn she actually forgot her terror of the cold so far as to remain out walking in the grounds of the palace, though the snow clouds were gathering thick and heavy overhead.

She was alone. For sometimes in

her saddest moods she could bear no one, not even the most faithful of her ladies, near her.

'If only I had a little baby, a dear little baby of my own, I would never complain of anything again.'

No doubt she quite meant what she said. And I must say if her only complaints had been of the cold northern winter, I could indeed find it in my heart to pity her—not that I have any experience of them myself (and the bird gave a little shiver), but I can imagine how terrible they must be. Indeed the friend from whom I have this story has often described his sufferings to me, one year when he was belated in the north, owing to an injured wing. That is how he came to know the story.

As the Queen uttered her wish, she raised her eyes upwards, and was startled to see some snowflakes already falling; she turned to hasten indoors, exclaiming as she went:

"GLANCING UP, THE QUEEN SAW A
LOVELY FIGURE."

'To think that winter is upon us already; I shall no longer have even the small pleasure of a stroll in the garden. But if I had a little baby to play with and care for, even the dreary winter would not seem long. Everything would be bright and sunshiny to me.'

'Are you sure of that?' said a voice beside her, and glancing up the Queen saw a lovely figure. It was that of a beautiful woman, with golden hair wreathed with flowers. But her face was somewhat pale and she drew round her a mantle of russet brown as if to protect her from the cold.

'I am the Spirit of the Summer,' she said. 'I knew you well in your childhood in the south, and here too I have watched you, though you did not know it. Your wish shall be fulfilled. When I return to my northern home, I will bring you the child you are longing for. But remember, the gift will lead to no lasting happiness unless you overcome your habit of discontent. For I can only do my part. My brother, the powerful Spirit of the Winter, though good and true and faithful, is stern and severe. He has heard your murmurings already, and if, when your great wish is granted, you still continue them, I tremble for the fate of your child.'

The Queen could hardly speak, so overcome was she with delight.

'Thank you, oh, thank you, sweet spirit,' she said. 'I will indeed take heed for the future and never murmur again.'

'I trust so,' replied the fairy, 'for listen what will happen if you forget your resolution. The slightest touch of snow would, in that case, put the baby into my stern brother's power, and you would find yourself terribly punished. Beware, therefore! Now I must hasten away. I have lingered too long this year, and though my brother and I work together and trust

each other, he brooks no interference.'
And as she said this, the gracious figure
seemed to disappear in a rosy haze,
and almost at the same moment a cold
blast, driving the snowflakes before it,
came with a rush from behind where
the young Queen stood, almost lifting
her from her feet.

'That must surely be the Spirit of
the Winter himself,' she thought as she
hurried indoors.

But her cheeks were rosy and her
eyes bright. It was whispered in the
palace that evening that for the first
time the young Queen had the brave
and fearless air of a true daughter of
the north. And that winter was far
the happiest that the King and his wife
had yet spent. Scarce a murmur was
heard to escape from the Queen's lips,
and in her anxiety to win the good-will
of the Winter Spirit, she often went
out sleighing and joined in the other
amusements which hitherto she had
refused to take any part in during

the cold season. More than once, even, she was heard to express admiration of the snow-covered mountains, or of the wonderful northern sunsets and clear star-bespangled skies.

Nevertheless, the return of the warm and sunny days was watched for by her most eagerly. And the Summer Spirit was true to her promise. On the loveliest morning of all that year was born a baby Princess, the prettiest baby that ever was seen, with dark-blue eyes and little golden curls all over her head.

'A true child of the summer,' said the happy Queen.

'And strong to brave and enjoy the winter too, I trust,' added the King. 'She must be a true Princess of the north, as her mother is fast becoming, I hope,' he went on with a smile.

But his words did not please the Queen, though they were so kindly meant. With the possession of the baby, though she was so overjoyed to have her, the young Queen's wayward and dissatisfied spirit began to return. She seemed to think the Princess was to be only hers, that the nation and even the King, who naturally felt they had a share in her, must give way, in everything that concerned the child, to its mother's will.   She was even displeased one day when she overheard some of her ladies admiring the beautiful colour of the baby's hair and saying that it showed her a true daughter of the north.

'No such thing,' said the Queen. 'It shows her a child of the sunshine and the summer.   My sweet Rose!' for so, to please the Queen, the baby had been named.

On the whole, however, while the summer lasted the Queen was too happy with her baby to give way to any real murmuring, and once or twice when she might perhaps have done so, there was wafted to her by the breeze the sound of a gentle 'Beware!' and she knew that the summer fairy was near.'

So for the first winter of the baby's life she was on her guard, and nothing went wrong, except now and then when the King reproached his wife with over-care of the child when the weather was at all severe.

' Do you wish to kill her ? ' the Queen would reply, angrily.

' I wish to make her brave and hardy, like all the daughters of our race,' replied the King.

But not wishing to distress his wife, he said no more, reflecting that it would be time enough when the little girl could walk and run to accustom her to the keen and bracing air of the northern winter.

But in some strange, mysterious way, the princess, baby though she was, seemed to understand what her father felt about her. It was noticed that before she could speak at all, she would dance in her nurse's arms and stretch out her little hands with glee at the sight of the snowflakes falling steadily.

And once or twice when a draught of
the frosty air blew upon her she laughed
with delight, instead of shrinking or
shivering.

But so well were the Queen's feelings
understood that no one ventured to
tell her of these clear signs that little
Rose felt herself at home in the land
of the snow.

CHAPTER VIII

THE SUMMER PRINCESS (*continued*)

THE winter passed and the summer came again—the second summer of the baby's life. She had grown like the flowers, and was as happy as the butterflies. Never was a sweeter or a merrier child. The Queen idolised her, and the King loved her quite as dearly, though in a wiser way. And that summer passed very happily.

Unfortunately, however, the warm fine days came to an end unusually early that year. Many of the birds took flight for the south sooner than

their wont, and the flowers drooped
and withered as if afraid of what was
coming.

The Queen noticed these signs with
a sinking heart. Standing one chilly
morning at the palace windows, she
watched the gray autumn sky and
sighed deeply.

'Alas, alas!' she said. 'All the
beauty and brightness are going again.'

She did not know that the King had
entered the room, and was standing
behind her.

'Nay,' he said, cheerfully. 'You
have no reason to feel so sad. If you
have no other flower you have our
little Rose, blooming as brightly in the
winter as in the warmth.'

He meant it well, but it would have
been wiser if he had said nothing.
The Queen turned towards him impatiently.

'It is not so,' she said angrily.
'Rose is like me. She loves the
summer and the sunshine! I do not

I

believe she would live through your
wretched northern winters but for my
incessant care and constant watchful-
ness.   And the anxiety is too much
for me ; it will wear me to death before she is grown up.   Indeed there
are times when I almost regret that
she ever was born.   The life in this
country is but half a life.   Would that
I had known it before I ever came
hither.'

It was rarely, discontented and com-
plaining though she was, that the
Queen had so yielded to her temper.
The King was deeply hurt and disappointed, and he left the room without speaking.   He was generally so
kind and patient that this startled her,
and brought her to her senses.

' How wrong of me to grieve him so
by my wild words,' she thought, peni-
tently. ' And——'   A sudden horror
came over her.   What had she been
saying ?   What had she done ?   And
the fairy's warning returned to her

memory: 'If you forget your resolution, the slightest touch of snow will put the baby into my stern brother's power, and you will find yourself terribly punished.'

The poor Queen shivered. Already to her excited fancy, as she glanced at the sky, it seemed that the lurid gray which betokened snow was coming over it.

'Oh, sweet Summer Spirit!' she cried; 'forgive me and plead for me.'

But a melancholy wail from the cold wind blowing through the trees in the grounds of the palace was the only reply; the summer fairy was far away.

The sky cleared again later that day, and for some short time the cold did not increase. But it would be difficult to describe what the Queen went through. It was useless to hope that the winter would pass without snow; for, so far north, such a thing had never been known. Still, no

doubt, its coming appeared to be de-
layed, and the weather prophets felt
somewhat at fault. The Queen began
to breathe rather more freely again,
in the hope that possibly her appeal
to the Summer Spirit had, after all,
been heard. Every one had noticed
her pale and anxious looks; every one
had noticed also how very gentle and
uncomplaining she had become. She
was so eager to make all the amends
she could, that one day, when the
King remarked that he thought it
very wrong for the Princess to be
so guarded from the open air as she
had been lately, the Queen, though
with fear and trembling, gave orders
that the baby should be taken out.

'I will accompany her myself,' she
said to the attendants; so the little
Princess was wrapped up in her costly
furs and placed in her tiny chariot
drawn by goats, the Queen walking
beside her.

The little girl laughed with delight,

and chattered in her baby way about everything she saw. She seemed like a little prisoner suddenly set at liberty; for the last few weeks had been spent by the poor little thing in rooms specially prepared, where no breath of the outer air could find its way in.

'For who knows,' thought the Queen, 'how some tiny flake of snow might be wafted down the chimney, or through the slightest chink of the window.'

To-day, in spite of her anxiety, the baby's happy face made her mother's heart feel lighter.

'Surely,' she said to herself, 'it must be a sign that I am forgiven, and that all will yet be well.'

And to please her little daughter she took her farther than she had intended, even entering a little way into a pine wood skirting the palace grounds at one side, a favourite resort of hers in the summer.

The Princess's nurse picked up

some fir-cones and gave them to the
little girl, who threw them about in
glee and called out for more. They
were all so busy playing with her
that they did not notice how, above
the heads of the tall fir-trees, the sky
was growing dark and overcast, till
suddenly a strange, chill blast made
the Queen gather her mantle round
her and gaze up in alarm.

'We must hasten home,' she said;
'it is growing so cold.'

'Yes, indeed,' said one of the ladies;
'it almost looks like——' But the
Queen interrupted her; she could not
bear even the mention of the fatal
word.

'Wrap up the Princess!' she exclaimed. 'Cover her over, face and
all! Never mind if she cries! My
darling, we shall be home directly.
The cold wind would hurt you,' added
she to the little girl.

Then they hurried back to the palace
as quickly as the goats could be per-

suaded to go, even the Queen herself
running fast to keep up with the little
carriage.

They were within a short distance
of the palace before any snow fell,
though it was clear to be seen that
it was not far off; and the Queen
was beginning to breathe again more
freely, when suddenly Princess Rose,
who had behaved beautifully till now,
with a cry of baby mischief, pushed
away the shawl that was over her
face, shouting with glee. At that
very moment the first fluttering snowflakes began to fall. The little Princess opened wide her eyes as she
caught sight of them, and smiled as
if in greeting; and alas! before the
terrified Queen had time to replace
the covering the child had thrown
off, one solitary flake alighted on her
cheek, melting there into a tiny drop
which looked like a tear, though still
the little Princess smiled.

The Queen seized the child in her

arms, and, though her heart had almost
ceased beating with terror, rushed up
the long flights of steps, all through
the great halls and corridors like a
mad creature, nor stopped even to
draw breath till she had reached the
Princess's apartments, and had her
safe in the rooms specially prepared
for her during the winter.

But was she safe? Was it not
already too late? With trembling
dread the Queen drew away the furs
and shawls wrapped round the baby,
almost expecting to find her changed
in some strange way, perhaps even
dead; and it was with thankfulness
that she saw that little Rose was still
herself—sweet and smiling in her sleep.
For she was fast asleep.

'The darling, the precious angel,'
thought the poor mother as she laid
her in her little cot, just as the ladies,
and nurses, and all the attendants came
trooping into the room. 'She is only
asleep,' said the Queen, in a whisper.

'Nothing has happened to her—she is sleeping sweetly.'

The ladies stared—the Queen's behaviour had been so strange they could not understand her.

'It is a pity to be so anxious about the child,' they said to each other. 'It will bring no blessing,' for they thought it all came from the Queen's foolish terror lest the little Princess should catch cold, and they shook their heads.

But the Queen seemed full of thankfulness, very gentle, and subdued. Many times that afternoon she came back to see if little Rose was well—the baby looked a picture of health, but— she was still sleeping.

'The fresh keen air has made her drowsy, I suppose,' said the head nurse, late in the evening when the Queen returned again.

'And she has had nothing to eat since the middle of the day,' said the mother, anxiously. 'I almost think if she does

not wake of herself in an hour or so,
you will have to rouse her.'

To this the nurse agreed. But two
hours later, on the Queen's next visit
to the nursery, there was a strange
report to give her. The nurse had
tried to wake the baby, but it was
all in vain. Little Rose just smiled
sweetly and rolled over on her
other side, without attempting in the
least to open her eyes. It seemed
cruel to disturb her. She was so
very sleepy.

'I think we must let the Princess
have her sleep out—children are like
that sometimes,' said the nurse.

And the Queen was forced to agree
to it, though she had a strange sinking
at the heart, and even the King when
he came to look at his little daughter
felt uneasy, though he tried to speak
cheerfully.

'No doubt she will awake in the
morning quite bright and merry,' he
said,—'all the brighter and merrier for

sleeping a good round and a half of the clock.'

The morning dawned—the slow-coming winter daylight of the north found its way into the Princess's nursery through the one thickly glazed window —a tiny gleam of ruddy sunshine even managed to creep in to kiss her dimpled cheek, but still the baby slept—as soundly as if the night was only beginning. And matters grew serious.

It was no use trying to wake her. They all did their best—King, Queen, ladies, nurses; and after them the great court physicians and learned men of every kind. All were summoned and all consulted, and as the days went on, a hundred different things were tried. They held the strongest smelling salts to her poor little nostrils; the baby only drew up her small nose the least bit in the world and turned over again with a tiny snore. They rang the bells, they had the loudest German bands to be found far

or near to play all at once in her
room; they fetched all the pet dogs
in the neighbourhood and set them
snarling and snapping at each other
close beside her; as a last resource
they lifted her out of bed and
plunged her into a cold bath—she did
not even shiver!

And with tears rolling down their
faces, the Queen and the ladies and
the nurses wrapped her up again and
put her back cosily to bed, where she
seemed as contented as ever, while
they all sat down together to have a
good cry, which, sad to say, was of no
use at all.

'She is bewitched,' said the
cleverest of all the doctors, and as
time went on, everybody began to
agree with him. Even the King
himself was obliged to think something of the kind must be at the bottom
of it, and at last one day the Queen,
unable to endure her remorse any
longer, told him the whole story,

entreating him to forgive her for
having by her discontent and murmuring brought upon him so great a
sorrow.

The King was very kind but very
grave.

'I understand it now,' he said.
'The summer fairy told you true. Our
northern Winter Spirit is indeed stern
and implacable; we must submit—if
we are patient and resigned it is
possible that in the future even his
cold heart may be melted by the sight
of our suffering.'

'It is only I who deserve it,' wept
the poor Queen. 'The worst part of
it all is to know that I have brought
this sorrow upon you, my dear
husband.'

And so repentant was she that she
almost forgot to think of herself—
never had she been so sweet and
loving a wife. She did everything
she possibly could to please and cheer
the King, concealing from him the

many bitter tears she shed as she sat for hours together beside the sleeping child.

The winter was terribly severe— never had the snow lain more thickly, never had the wind-blasts raged and howled more furiously. Often did the Queen think to herself that the storm spirits must be infuriated at her very presence in their special domain.

'They might pity me now,' she thought, 'now that I am so punished;' but she bore all the winter cold and terrors uncomplainingly, nay, even cheerfully, nerving herself to go out alone in the bitterest weather with a sort of hope of pleasing the winter fairy; possibly if she could but see him, of making an appeal to him. But for many months he held his icy sway —often indeed it seemed as if gentler times were never to return.

Then suddenly one night the frost went; a mild soft breeze replaced the fierce blast; spring had come. And

wonderful to relate, the very next
morning the Queen was roused by
loud knockings and voices at her door;
trembling, she knew not why, she
opened it; and the head nurse fell at
her feet laughing and crying at once.
The Princess had awakened!

Yes; there she was, chattering in
her baby way, smiling and rosy, as if
nothing had been the matter. She
held out her arms to her mother, calling 'Mamma,' in the most delightful
way; she knew her father again quite
well; she was very hungry for her
breakfast. Oh! the joy of her parents,
and the jubilation all through the
palace! I could not describe it.

And all through the summer little
Rose was wide awake, in the day-time
that is to say, just like other children.
She was as well and strong and happy
as a baby could be. But — the
summer will not last for ever; again
returned the autumn bringing with it
the signs of the approaching winter,

and one morning when her nurse went to awaken the Princess, she found it was no use—Rose was sleeping again, with a smile on her face, calm and content, but alas! not to be awakened! And then it was remembered that the first snow had fallen during the night.

More to satisfy the Queen than with the hope of its doing any good, all the efforts of the year before were repeated, but with no success. And gradually the child's distressed parents resigned themselves to the sad truth : their daughter was to be theirs only for half her life; for full six months out of every twelve, she was to be in a sense as far away from them as if the winter monarch had carried her off to his palace of ice altogether.

But no; it was not quite so bad as that would have been. And the Queen, who was fast learning to count her blessings instead of her troubles, smiled through her tears as she said to the King what a mercy it was that

they were still able to watch beside
their precious child—to kiss her soft
warm cheek every morning and every
night.

And so it went on. In the spring
the Princess woke up again, bright
and well and lively, and in every way
six months older than when she had
fallen asleep; so that, to see her in
the summer time, no one could have
guessed the strange spell that was over
her. She became the sweetest and
most charming girl in the world; only
one thing ever saddened her, and that
was any mention of the winter, especially of snow.

'What does it mean?' she would
ask sometimes. 'What are they talking
of? Show me this wonderful thing!
Where does it grow? I want to
see it.'

But no one could make her understand; and at these times a very strange
look would come into her blue eyes.

'I must see it,' she said. 'Some

day I shall go away and travel far, far,
till I find it.'

These words used to distress her
mother more. than she could say;
and she would shower presents and
treasures on her daughter, of flowers
and singing - birds, and lovely em-
broidered dresses—all to make her
think of the sunshine and the summer.
And for the time they would please
the girl, till again she shook her head
and murmured—'I want the snow.'

So the years followed each other,
till Rose was sixteen. Every winter
the Queen had a faint hope, which,
however, grew ever fainter and fainter,
that the spell was perhaps to be broken.
But it was not so. And strange stories
got about concerning the Princess—
some saying she was a witch in dis-
guise; others that she had no heart
or understanding; others that she
turned into a bird or some animal
during half her life — so that the
neighbouring Princes, in spite of her

beauty and sweetness, were afraid to ask her in marriage. And this brought new sorrow to her parents. For she was their only child.

'What will become of her after we are dead and gone?' they said. 'Who will care for and protect our darling? Who will help her to rule over our nation? No people will remain faithful to a sovereign who is only awake half the year. There will be revolts and rebellion, and our angel Rose may perhaps be put to death, or driven away.'

And they fretted so over this, that the hair of both King and Queen grew white long before its time. But Rose only loved them the more on this account, for she had heard some one say that white hair was like snow; though she kept the fancy to herself, for she knew it troubled the Queen if ever she mentioned the strange, mysterious word.

She was so lovely that painters came

from many countries just to see her face, and, if possible, be allowed to make a picture of her. And one of these portraits found its way to the court of a King who was a distant cousin of her father, and who had heard the strange things said of the Princess. He was very angry about it, for he had two sons, and he was afraid of their falling in love with the beautiful face. So he ordered the picture to be destroyed before the elder Prince, who was away on a visit, came home.

But the servant who was to burn the picture thought it such a pity to do so, that he only hid it away in a lumber-room; and thither, as fate would have it, came the younger Prince one day in search of a pet kitten of his sister's which had strayed away; for he was a Prince of a most kind and amiable nature.

The moment he saw the picture he fell in love with it. He made

inquiry, and heard all there was to
tell. Then he arrayed himself for a
journey, and came to bid his father
farewell.

'I go,' he said, 'to woo the Princess Rose for my bride.' And in
spite of all the king could say he kept
firm.

'If she is a witch,' he said, 'I would
rather perish by her hands than live
with any other.'

And amidst tears and lamentations
he set out.

He was received with great delight
at the court of Princess Rose's
parents, though he came without
any pomp or display; for he lost no
time in telling the King and Queen
the reason of his visit. Knowing him
to be a Prince of most estimable
character, they were overjoyed to hear
of his resolve.

'I only trust,' said the Queen, 'that
all may go well. But, as you have
doubtless heard, our darling child,

despite her beauty and goodness, is
under a strange spell.'

She then proceeded to tell him the
whole matter, of which he had already
heard garbled accounts.

He was relieved to find that the
enchantment was of no worse a nature,
and declared that it made no difference
in his intentions, but rather increased
his love for the Princess.   And when
he first set eyes on her (more beautiful
by far than even the beautiful portrait),
he felt that his whole life would not
be too much to devote to her, even
considering her strange affliction.

'And who knows,' he said to himself,
'but that such love as mine may find out
a way to release her from the spell?'

The Princess quickly learned to like
him.   She had never before had a
companion so near her own age, and
the last days of the summer passed
most happily, till the time came when
the Prince thought he might venture
to ask her to be his wife.

They were walking on the terrace
in front of the castle when he did
so. It had been a lovely day, but
the afternoon had grown chilly; and
as the Princess listened to his words,
a cold breath of wind passed near
them.

The Princess started; and, aware
of the Queen's anxiety about her,
the Prince hastily proposed that they
should return to the house; but Rose
looked at him with a light in her
eyes which he had never before seen,
and a strange smile broke over her face.

'It is new life to me,' she said.
'Can you not understand, you who
are yourself a child of the north?
Yes, Prince, I will marry you on one
condition, that you will show me the
snow—but on no other.'

Then she turned, and, without
another word, walked slowly back to
the palace.

Prince Orso, for so he was called,
felt terribly distressed.

'The spell is upon her,' he thought
to himself. 'She asks me to do what
would probably kill her, or separate
her for ever from all who love her.'

And the King and Queen, when
they heard his story, were nearly as
disappointed as he.

But that very night the Prince had
a strange dream. He thought he was
walking in the wood near the castle,
when again a chill blast, but still more
icy, swept past him, and he heard a
voice speaking to him. It sounded
hoarse and stern.

'Orso,' it said, 'you're as foolish as
the rest. Have you no trust? See
what came of rebellion against me,
who, after all, love my many children
as dearly as does my sister of the
summer. Leave the Princess to the
leadings of her own heart, and dare
not to interfere.'

Then with a crash as of thunder the
spirit went on his way. And the
Prince awoke to find that the window

of his room had been dashed in by the force of a sudden gale which had arisen.

But the next morning all was again calm. It almost seemed as if the milder weather was returning again; and the Queen looked brighter; but it was not so with the Princess, who was silent and almost sad. And so things continued for some days.

At last the Prince could bear it no longer. One afternoon when he found himself alone with the Princess, he turned to her suddenly.

'Princess,' he said, 'can you not give me another answer? You must know that I would fain promise any- thing you wish; but I dare not bind myself to what might perhaps do you some injury.'

Rose turned towards him impatiently.

'That is just it,' she said. 'I am always met by excuses when I ask for the one thing I really desire. What is there about me different from others? Why should I so often hear of what others seem to understand, and not have it explained to me? I am no longer a child; in my dreams I see things I cannot put in words; and beautiful as the world is, I feel that I only half know it. I long for what they call the winter, and what they call the snow, and they never come. Only the cold wind, which I have felt once or twice, brings new life to me, and fills me with strange joy.'

The Prince hesitated. He understood her perfectly, for he was himself of the same brave and hardy race. Yet the Queen's forebodings made him tremble. The Princess's words reminded him of his own dream; and again he felt as if he heard the voice of the stern Winter Spirit. And as if in answer to his uncertainty, at that moment the howl of the cold blast sounded near them among the trees, and lurid clouds began to gather overhead.

The Princess's face lighted up.

'Ah,' she exclaimed, 'it is coming again !'

'I fear so indeed,' said Orso; and in his terror for her he caught her hand and would have hurried her back to the palace.

But at that moment a shrill little cry was heard overhead not far from where they stood, and glancing up they saw a bird of prey clutching a smaller one in his claws. With a terrible effort the captive managed to free himself, but he was sadly wounded; and as Rose gazed upwards in great concern, she saw him fall fluttering feebly to the ground. All else was forgotten in the sight.

'Poor bird,' she cried. 'Let me go, Prince; I must find him where he has fallen, or a cruel death of slow suffering will be his.'

The Prince loosed her hand; he dared not hold her back, though he could have done so.

'Leave her to the guidings of her own heart,' resounded in his ears.

Almost at once she was lost to his sight among the trees which grew very closely; almost at the same moment, to his horror, something cold and soft touched his face, and lifting his eyes, he saw that the snowflakes were falling thickly. If harm was to betide, it was too late to save her; but he pressed forward in unspeakable anxiety.

It was some little time before he found her; and no reply came to his calls; but at last he caught sight of something blue on the ground. It was the Princess's robe; and there, indeed, she lay motionless—her eyes closed, a sweet smile on her face, the little wounded bird tenderly clasped in her hands.

And now I may tell you that this wounded bird was the friend from whom I had the story; for, as you will hear, he had plenty of opportunity of learning it all.

Orso threw himself on the ground beside the Princess.

'Ah,' he exclaimed, 'my carelessness has killed her. How can I ever dare to face the King and Queen? Oh! Winter Spirit, you have indeed deceived me.'

But as he said the words the Princess opened her eyes.

'No, Prince,' she said. 'I am not dead. I am not even asleep. It was the strange gladness that seemed to take away my breath for a moment, and I must have sunk down without knowing. But now I feel stronger and happier than ever in my life before, now that I have seen and felt the beautiful snow of my own country, now that I have breathed the winter air I have been longing for always,' and she sprang to her feet, her blue eyes sparkling with delight, looking lovelier than he had ever seen her.

'Orso,' she went on, half shyly, 'you have done what I asked you; through you I have seen the snow,' and she held out her hand, which, white though it was, looked pink in comparison with the little flakes which were fluttering down on it.

The Prince was overjoyed, but he hesitated.

'I fear,' he said, 'that in reality you should rather thank the poor little bird, or most of all your own kind heart.'

'Poor little bird,' she replied, looking at it as it lay in her other hand. 'It is not dead. I will do all I can for it! Let us hasten home, Prince, so that I may bind up its poor wing. My father and mother too will be anxious about me.'

And together they returned to the palace. One glance at the Princess as she came in sprinkled over with snow showed the Queen that the spell was at last broken. And her joy was past all words.

My friend recovered slowly. He spent all the winter in the palace,

tenderly cared for by the Princess Rose,
only flying away when the warm sunny
days returned. He pays them a visit still
every summer to show his gratitude,
and tells me that in all his travels he
seldom sees a happier family than his
friends in the old palace away up in the
far, far northern land.

'Thank you,' said the children,
'Thank you, oh so much!' But whether
the bird heard them or not they could
not tell—he had already flown away.

CHAPTER IX

THE CHRISTMAS SURPRISE

FOR some days the story of the bewitched Princess gave Rafe and Alix enough to talk about, and to play at too, for they invented a game in which Alix was supposed to fall into an enchanted sleep if Rafe succeeded in touching her with a branch of leaves, which represented snowflakes; and as she was a very quick runner it was not so easy as it sounds.

Besides, by this time the Easter holidays were over and lessons had begun again. The children had not

too many lessons, however, and always
a good part of the afternoon to themselves, and they remained faithful to the
old garden as their favourite playground.
So some hours of every day—of every
fine day at least—were spent there, and
though they had not seen the old caretaker a second time, nor ever managed
to find the concealed door in the rough
stone wall again, hunt for it as they
would, still they had sometimes a queer,
mysterious, pleasant feeling that she
knew about them—knew they were
there, and was perhaps even peeping
out at them through some hidden hole.

It would have been a great sorrow
to them if they had had to give up their
visits to the garden. But fortunately
their nurse rather approved of their
playing there. There was something
that brought good luck with it about
the Ladywood grounds. No ill-chance
ever happened to them there, no
tumbles or sprained ankles, or torn
clothes, or such not uncommon mis-

fortunes when children are by themselves. Best of all, they almost never
quarrelled when in the old garden, and
perhaps *that* had a good deal to do with
the keeping clear of other troubles.

They were growing 'quite to be
trusted,' nurse told their mother, and it
scarcely seemed needful for them to go
regular walks now, which nurse was very
glad of, as it left her free to get on nicely
with all the needlework, in which—
next to a baby, and there had been
no new baby since Alix—her heart
delighted.

So the discovery of the pleasures of
the deserted manor suited everybody.

But after a while, the children began
to think it was time to have another
story, and to wonder if their old friend
had forgotten them, or possibly gone
away. There was no use hunting any
more for the hidden door ; they had
hurt their fingers and tired themselves
to no purpose in doing so already.
And at last they came to the conclusion

that if Mrs. Caretaker didn't want them
to find it, it was no use trying, and that
if she *did*, she would soon find ways
and means of fetching them.

'Unless, of course,' said Alix, 'she
has gone. Perhaps she's like the birds,
you know—only turned the other way.
I mean perhaps she goes off in the
summer, once she's started everything,
and all the plants and things *are* growing
beautifully now, in their wild way. You
see she's not like a regular trim gardener
—she doesn't want them to grow all
properly like you can see anywhere.'

'Still she must take great care of
them somehow,' said Rafe thoughtfully,
'for you know people often notice how
 ew weeds there are about Ladywood,
and in full summer the wild flowers
are quite wonderful. And the birds—
it's always here the nightingales are
heard the best.'

Alix looked up. They were sitting
in their favourite place, at the foot of
some very tall trees.

'If we'd had any sense,' she said, 'we might almost have seen for ourselves long ago that there was something fairy about the place, even before the wren led us here.'

The mention of the wren made her remember something she had noticed.

'Rafe,' she went on, 'do you know I've seen a little robin hopping about us the last day or two, and chirping in a *talking* sort of way. I forgot to tell you. I wonder if he has anything to say to us, for you know there were *two* birds that wanted to tell us stories.'

'Per——' began Rafe in his slow fashion.

But before he had time to get to 'haps' his sister caught hold of his arm.

'Hush!' she whispered, 'there he is.'

Yes, there he was, and 'he' *was* a robin.

He hopped about in front of them for a minute or two, now and then cocking his head on one side and look-

ing at them over his shoulder, as it
were, as if to see whether he had
caught their attention. Then he flew
up a little way, and settled himself on
a branch not far from them, with a
peculiar little chirp.

'I believe,' said Alix, still in a whisper, 'I believe he wants us to speak to
him.'

'Try,' replied Rafe.

'Robin,' said Alix, clearly though
softly, 'robin, have you come to see
us? Have you got a message for us
from Mrs. Caretaker, perhaps?'

The bird looked at her reproachfully. I don't know that she could
see it was *reproachfully*, but from the
way he held his head it was plain to
any one that he was not altogether
pleased.

Then came a succession of chirps,
and gradually, just as had happened
before, by dint of listening very at-
tentively and keeping quite, quite quiet,
bits of words and then words them-

selves began to grow out of the chirping.   To tell the truth, if any one had
passed that way, he or she would have
imagined Rafe and Alix were asleep.
For there they sat, like a picture of the
babes in the wood—Alix's head resting
on her brother's shoulder, and his arm
thrown round her—*quite* motionless.
But they weren't asleep, of course, for
their two pairs of eyes were fixed on the
little redbreasted fellow up above them.

'So you had forgotten all about me,
in a melancholy tone, quite unlike a
cheery little robin.   'I gave up to that
other fellow and let him tell his story
first.   I suppose you don't care to hear
mine.'

'Oh, dear robin, of course we do,'
said Alix.   'But you see we didn't
understand.'

'I've been following you about all
these days.   I'm sure you might have
seen me, and I've been asking you
over and over again if you didn't want
to listen.'

' But you see, dear robin, we couldn't understand what you said. It takes a good while to get used to—to your way of speaking, you know,' said Alix. She was desperately afraid of hurting his feelings still more.

'I am afraid that is not the real reason. You think a robin's story is sure to be stupid. You see I am not one of those fine travelled fellows— the swallows and the martins, and all the rest of them—who spend the winter in the south and know such a lot of the world. I'm only a home bird. Here I was hatched and here I have lived, and mean to live till I die. It's quite true that my story is a very stupid one. I've made no fine acquaintances such as kings and queens and prin- cesses, and I've never visited at court, north or south either, so you know what you have to expect.'

He seemed rather depressed, but less offended than he had been.

' Please begin,' said Rafe. ' I'm sure

we shall like your story. We don't want always to hear the same kind.'

The robin cleared his throat.

'Such as it is,' he began, 'I can vouch for the truth of it, as it happened to be my own self. I didn't "have it" from any one else. And in my own mind I have given it the name of

'THE CHRISTMAS SURPRISE.'

And after he had cleared his throat again for the last time, he went straight on.

'I have often noticed,' he began, 'that whatever we have not got, whatever is not ours or with us at the present moment, is the thing we prize the most. This applies both to birds and human beings, and it is often the case about the seasons of the year. There is a great charm about absence. In the winter we are always looking forward to the spring and the summer;

in the hot summer we think of the
cool shady days of autumn, of the
cheerful fires and merry doings that
come with Christmas. I am speaking
especially of men and women and children just now, but there is a good
deal of the same kind of thing among
us birds, though you mightn't think it.
And of all birds, I think we robins
have the most sympathy with human
folk. We really love Christmas time;
it is gratifying to know how much we
are thought of at that season—how
our portraits are sent about by one
friend to another, how our figures are
placed on your Christmas trees, and
how every one thinks of us with kindness. And except by *very* thoughtless
people we are generally cared for well.
During a hard winter it is seldom that
our wants are forgotten. I myself,'
and here he plumed himself import-
antly, 'I myself have been most fortunate in this respect. There are at
least a dozen houses within easy flight

of Ladywood where I am always sure of a good breakfast of crumbs.'

'But,' began Alix, rather timidly, 'please don't mind my interrupting you, but doesn't Mrs. Caretaker look after you? I thought that was what she was here for, to take care of all the living creatures in this garden.'

'Exactly so, exactly so,' said the robin, hastily, 'far be it from me to make any complaint. I would not change my home for the garden of a palace. But, as I have said, I think we robins have much sympathy with your race. Human beings interest me extremely. I like to study their characters. So I go about in my own part of the country a good deal, and thus I know the ways of many of my wingless neighbours pretty intimately. Thus comes it that I have stories to tell, all from my own observation, you see. Well, as I was remarking, we often love to dwell in fancy on what is not ours at present, so as it is really like a

summer day, quite hot for the time of
year, I daresay it will amuse you to
transport your thoughts to Christmas
time. Most of my human stories
belong to that season, for it is then
we have so much to do with you.
The Christmas of which I am going to
tell you was what is called an "old-
fashioned one," — though it strikes
me that snowy, frosty, very cold Christ-
mases are fast becoming *new*-fashioned
again — ah, it *was* cold ! I was a
young bird then ; it was my first experience of frost and snow, and in
spite of my feathers I did shiver, I can
tell you. Still I enjoyed it ; I was
strong and hearty, and I began to
make acquaintance with the houses in
the neighbourhood, at several of which
one was pretty sure of a breakfast in
front of some window.

There was a very large house which
had been shut up for some time, as the
owners were abroad. It had a charming terrace in front, and my friends and

I often regretted that it was not inhabited. For the terrace faced south and all the sunshine going was sure to be found there, and it would have been a pleasant resort for us. And one morning our wishes were fulfilled. I met a cousin of mine flying off in great excitement.

'The Manor House is open again,' he told me. 'Come quickly. Through the windows on to the terrace, fires are to be seen in all the rooms, and they are evidently preparing for a merry Christmas. No doubt they will not forget us, but it is as well to remind them that we should be glad of some crumbs.'

I flew off with him, and found it just as he had said. The house had quite a different appearance; it looked bright and cheery, and in one room a large party was assembled at breakfast. We—for several of us were there—hopped up and down the terrace for some little time, but no notice was

taken of us.   So one by one my companions flew away, remarking that it
was no use wasting their time ; they
would look in again some other day
when perhaps the new-comers would
have thought of them.   But I remained behind ; I was not very busy,
being a young bird, and I felt a wish
to see something of the family who
had been so long absent, for I am of
what some people call a ' curious '
disposition ; I myself should rather
describe it as observant and thoughtful.

I perched close beside the dining-
room window and peeped in.   There
were several grown-up people, but only
two children ; two little girls, very
prettily dressed, but thin and pale, and
with a somewhat discontented expression of face.   After a while, when the
meal was over and all had risen from
the table, the children came to the
window with a young lady and stood
looking out.

' Oh, how cold it is,' said one of

them shivering, 'I wish papa and mamma had not come back to England. I liked India much better.'

'So did I,' said the other little girl. 'I don't want to go a walk when it's so cold. Need we go, Miss Meadows? And yet I don't know what to do in the house. I'm tired of all our toys. We shall have new ones next week when Christmas Day comes; that's a good thing.'

The young lady they called Miss Meadows looked rather troubled. In her heart she thought the children had far too many toys already, and she felt sure they would get tired of the new ones before they had had them long.

'I don't care much for Christmas except for the toys,' said the first little girl. 'Do you, Miss Meadows?'

'Yes, indeed I do, Norna dear,' she said. 'And I think in your heart you really care for it too—and Ivy also. You both know *why* it should be so cared for.'

'Oh, yes; in that sort of a way, I know it would be naughty not to care for it,' said Norna, looking a little ashamed. 'But it's different when you've lived in England, I suppose. Mamma has told us stories of Christmas when she was little, that sounded very nice—all about carols, and lots of cousins playing together, and presents, and school feasts. But we haven't any cousins to play with. Had you, Miss Meadows, at your own home?'

Miss Meadows' eyes looked rather odd for a moment. She turned away for half an instant and then she seemed all right again.

'I had lots of brothers and sisters,' she said, 'and that's even better than cousins.'

It was her first Christmas away from home, and she had only been a few days with Norna and Ivy.

'I wish we had!' sighed Norna, who always wanted what she had not got.

'But surely there are some things you can have that would cheer you up,' said Miss Meadows. 'Perhaps it is too soon to settle about school feasts just yet, but have you no presents to get ready for any one?'

'No,' sighed Ivy. 'Mamma has everything she wants; and so have we. It's rubbish giving each other presents just to say they're presents.'

'Yes,' said Miss Meadows. 'I think it is.   But——'

She said no more, for just then Ivy touched her, and whispered softly,

'I do believe there's a real little robin redbreast.   Don't let's frighten him away.'

The child's eyes sparkled with pleasure; she looked quite different.

'It's the first *real* one we've ever seen,' said she and Norna together.

'Poor little man!' said their governess; 'he must be hungry to be so tame.   Let us throw crumbs every morning, children.   I am sure your mamma won't mind. This terrace is a splendid place.'

The idea pleased them mightily. I hid myself in the ivy for a few moments, and when I came out again, there was a delightful spread all ready. So I flew down and began to profit by it, expressing my thanks, of course, in a well-bred manner. The window was still open, and I heard some words that Miss Meadows murmured to herself:

'I wish I could find out some little service for others that they could do, even this first Christmas,' she said. 'They would be so much happier, poor little things! Dear robin, I am even grateful to you for making me think of throwing out crumbs.'

She looked so sweet that my heart warmed to her, and I wished I could help her. And at that moment an idea struck me. You will soon hear what it was.

I had another visit to pay that

morning; indeed I had been on my
way to do so when the exciting news
about the Manor House attracted
me thither. But now I flew off, to
the little home where I was always
welcome. It was a very small cottage
at the outskirts of the same village
of which the home of the newly-
returned family was the great house.
In this cottage lived a couple and
their two children—a boy and a girl.
They had always been poor, but
striving and thrifty, so that the little
place looked bright and comfortable
though so bare, and the children tidy
and rosy. But now, alas! things had
changed for the worse. A bad acci-
dent to the father, who was a wood-
cutter, had entirely crippled him; and
though some help was given them,
it was all the poor mother could do
to keep out of the workhouse. I
made a point of visiting the cottage
every day; it cheered them up, and
there were generally some crumbs for

me. But this morning—not that it
mattered to me after my good breakfast at the Manor House—there were
none; and as I alighted on the sill
of the little kitchen and looked in,
everything was dull and cheerless.
No fire was lighted; the two children,
Jem and Joyce, sat crouched together
on the settle by the empty grate as
if to gain a little warmth from each
other. They looked blue and pinched,
and scarcely awake; but when they
saw me at the window they brightened
up a little.

'There's robin,' said Joyce. 'Poor
robin! we've nothing for you this
morning.'

A small pane was broken in the
window and pasted over with paper,
but a corner was torn, and so I could
hear what they said.

'No indeed,' said Jem; 'we've had
nothing ourselves—not since yesterday at dinner time. And it is so
cold.'

I stood still on one leg, and chirped that I was very sorry. I think they understood me.

'Mother's gone to Farmer Bantry's,' said Joyce, as if she was glad to have some one—'even a bird,' some folk who know precious little about us would say—to tell her troubles to. 'They're cleanin' up for Christmas, and she'll get a shillin', and maybe some broken victuals, she said. So we're tryin' to go to sleep again to make the time pass.'

'There was two sixpences yesterday,' said Jem, mournfully; 'and one would 'a got some coal, and t'other some bread and tea. But the doctor said as father must have somefin'—' (Jem was only five and Joyce eight)—'queer stuff—I forget the name—to wunst. So mother she went to the shop, and father's got the stuff, and he's asleep; but we've not had nuffin'.'

'And Christmas is coming next week, mother says,' Joyce added.

'Last Christmas we had new shoes, and meat for dinner.'

I was sadly grieved for them. Joyce spoke in a dull, broken sort of tone that did not sound like a child. But I hoped to serve them better than by standing there repeating my regret; so, after a few more chirps of sympathy, I flew off.

'Robin doesn't care to stay,' said Jem, dolefully.

Later in the day I met the children's mother trudging home. She looked tired; but she had a basket on her arm, so I hoped the farmer's wife had given them some scraps which would help them for the time.

Now I had a plan in my head. Late that afternoon, after flying all round the Manor House and peeping in at a great many windows, I perched in the ivy—there was ivy over a great part of the walls—just outside one on the first floor. It was the children's bedroom. I waited anxiously, afraid

that I might have no chance of getting
in; but fortunately for me the fire
smoked a little when it was lighted
in the evening for the young ladies
to be dressed by, and the nurse
opened the window a tiny bit, so in
I flew, very careful not to be seen,
you may be sure. I found a very
cosy corner on the edge of a picture
in a dark part of the room, and there
I had time for a nap before Norna
and Ivy came to bed. Then when
all was silent for the night, I flew
down and took up my quarters on
the rail at the head of Norna's
bed; and when I had spent an hour
or so beside her, I gently fluttered
across to her sister; and though I
was chirping nearly all the time, my
voice was so low that no one entering
the room would have noticed it; or if
they had done so, they would probably
have thought it a drowsy cricket, half
aroused by the pleasant warmth of the
fire.

But my chirping did more than
soothe my little friends' slumbers
(and here the robin cocked his head
afresh and looked very solemn). Children (he said), human beings know
very little about themselves. You
don't know, for instance, anything
at all about yourselves when you're
asleep, or what dreams really are.
You speak of being 'sleepy,' or half-
asleep, as if it meant something very
stupid; whereas, sometimes when you
are whole asleep, you are much wiser
than when you are awake. Now it
is not my business to teach you things
you're perhaps not meant to understand at present, but this I can tell
you—if I perched on your pillows at
night when you're asleep, and chirped
in my own way to you, you'd have
no difficulty in understanding me.
And this was what happened to the
two little maidens a few nights before
their first Christmas in England. They
thought they had had a wonderful

dream—each of them separately, and
they never knew that the robin who
flew out of the window early in the
morning before any one noticed him,
had had anything to do with it.

I (for it was I myself, of course)
perched again in the ivy beside the
dining-room window, *partly*, I allow,
with a view to breakfast; partly and
principally to see what would happen.

They did not forget me—us, perhaps
I should say, for several other birds
collected on the terrace, thanks to the
news I had scattered about—and as
soon as those within had risen from
table, Miss Meadows and her two
little companions came to the window,
which they opened, and threw out a
splendid plateful of crumbs. It was
not so cold this morning. I hopped
close to them, for I wanted to hear
what they were saying as they stood
by the open window - door, all the
grown-up people having left the room.

The pale little faces looked bright

and eager, and very full of something
their owners were relating.

'Yes, Miss Meadows; it was quite
wonderful. Ivy dreamed it, and I
dreamed it. I believe it was a fairy
dream.'

'And please do let us try to find
out if there are any poor children like
that near here,' said Ivy. 'I don't
think there *could* be; do you, Miss
Meadows?'

Miss Meadows shook her head.

'I'm afraid, dear, it is not uncommon in either town or country to find
children quite as poor as those you
dreamt of. But when we go out a
walk to-day, we'll try and inquire a
little. It would be nice if you could
do something for other people even
this first Christmas in England.'

She looked quite bright and eager
herself; and as the three started off
down the drive about an hour later,
on their way to the village, I noticed
that they were all talking eagerly, and

that Norna and Ivy were giving little springs as they walked along one on each side of their kind governess; and I must confess I felt pleased to think I had had some hand in this improvement.

Miss Meadows had lived most of her life in the country, and she was accustomed to country ways. So she meant to go to the village, and there try to pick up a little information about any of the families who might be very poor this Christmas time. But I had no intention of letting them go so far—no indeed—I knew what I was about.

The cottage of my little friends, Joyce and Jem, was about half-way between the Manor House and the village, and the village was a good mile from the great house. A lane led from the high road to the cottage. Just as the three reached the corner of the lane, Ivy gave a little cry.

'Miss Meadows, Norna,' she said,

'there is the robin. I'm sure it's our robin. Don't you think it is, Miss Meadows?'

The governess smiled.

'There are a great many robins, Ivy dear. It's not very likely it's the same one. We human beings are too stupid to tell the difference between birds of the same kind, you see.'

But, as *you* know, Ivy was right.

'Do let's follow him a little way down the lane,' she said. 'He keeps hopping on and then looking back at us. I wonder if his home is down here.'

No, it was not *my* home, but it was my little friends' home; and soon I managed to bring the little party to a standstill before the cottage gate, where I had perched.

'What a nice cottage,' said Norna; and so it looked at the first glance. But in a moment or two she added: 'Oh, do look at that little girl; how very thin and pale she is!'

It was Joyce. Miss Meadows called
to her ; and in her kind way soon got
the little girl to tell her something of
their troubles. Things were even worse
with them to-day ; for Jem's feet were
so bad with chilblains that he could
not get about at all. The governess
satisfied herself that there was no
illness in the cottage that could hurt
Norna and Ivy, and then they all went
in to see poor Jem ; and Miss Meadows
went upstairs to speak to the bed-
ridden father. When she came down
again her face looked very sad, but
bright too.

'Children,' she said, as soon as they
were out on the road again, 'I don't
think we need go on to the village.
We have found what we were looking
for.'

Then she went on to tell them that
she had left a message with the wood-
cutter, asking his wife to come up to
speak to her that evening at the Manor
House.

'I know your mamma won't mind,' she said. 'I will tell her all about it as soon as we get home. She will like you to try to do something for these poor children'—which was quite true. The lady of the Manor was kind and gentle; only, you see, many years in India had got her out of English ways.

So that evening, when the wood-cutter's wife came up to the great house, there was a grand consultation. And for some days to come, for Christmas was very near, Ivy and Norna were so busy that they had no time to grumble at the cold or to wish they were back in India, though they did find time to skip and dance along the passages, and to sing verses of the carols Miss Meadows was teaching them.

Things improved at the cottage from that day. But it is about Christmas morning I want to tell you.

Joyce and Jem woke early—long

before it was light—but they lay still
and spoke in a whisper, not to wake
their poor father or their tired mother.
There was no one to hear except a
little robin, who had managed to creep
in the night before.

'It's Christmas, Jem,' said Joyce;
'and we shall have a nice fire. They've
sent mother some coals from the great
house; and I *believe* we're going to
have meat for dinner.'

Jem sighed with pleasure. He could
scarcely believe it.

'Shall we go to church like last
Christmas, Joyce?' he asked. 'My
boots is so drefful bad, I don't know
as I could walk in them.'

'So's mine,' said Joyce. 'But
p'r'aps if the roads is very dry, we
might manage.'

And so they chattered, till at last
the first rays of winter daylight began
to find their way into the little room.
The children looked about them—
somehow they had a feeling that things

could not look *quite* the same on
Christmas morning! But what they
did see was something very wonderful.
On the floor near the window were
two *very* big brown paper parcels; and
Joyce jumping out of bed to see what
they were, saw that to each was pinned
a card; and on one card was written,
'Joyce,' on the other, 'Jem.'

'*Jem*,' she cried, 'it must be fairies,'
and with trembling fingers they undid
the packages.

It is difficult to tell you their
delight!

There was a new frock of warm
linsey for Joyce, and a suit of corduroy
for Jem, boots for both—stockings and
socks—two splendid red comforters,
one knitted by Ivy and one by Norna;
a picture book for each, a bag of
oranges, and a beautiful home-made
cake.

Never were children so wild with
joy; never had there been such a
Christmas surprise.

I was so pleased that I could not remain hidden any longer. Out I came, and perching on the window-sill, warbled a Christmas carol in my own way. And I must say children are very quick.

'Dear robin,' said Joyce; 'do you know, Jem, I do believe he's a fairy! I shouldn't wonder if he'd somehow told the kind little young ladies to come and see us.'

There was a pause. Rafe and Alix waited a moment to make sure that the robin had quite finished; then they looked up. He was not in such a hurry to fly off as the other bird had been.

'Thank you *very* much, dear robin,' they said. 'It is a very pretty story indeed; and then it's so nice to know it's quite true.'

The robin looked pleased.

'Yes,' he said, 'there's that to be said for it. It's a very simple, homely story; but it's my own experience. But now I think I must bid you good-bye for the present, though there's no saying but what we may meet again.'

He flew off.

'Rafe,' said Alix, 'besides all the things mamma does and lets us help in sometimes for the poor people, wouldn't it be nice if we found some children we could do things for, more our own selves, you know?'

'Yes,' Rafe agreed, 'I think it would be.'

N

CHAPTER X

THE MAGIC ROSE

THE days and weeks and months went on, till it was full summer time again; more than full summer indeed. For it was August, and in a day or two Rafe and Alix were to go to the seaside for several weeks. They were very pleased of course, but still there is always a *little* sad feeling at 'going away,' especially from one's own home, even though it is only for a short time. They went all round the garden saying good-bye, as well as to the stables and the poultry yard and all the familiar places.

Then a sudden thought struck Alix.

'Rafe,' she said—it was the very evening before they left—'do let's say good-bye to the old garden too. And perhaps if we stood close to the corner of the wall and called through very loud, *perhaps* Mrs. Caretaker would hear us. It seems so funny that we've never seen her again. I think she *must* be away.'

'I don't know, I'm sure,' Rafe replied. ' I've sometimes had a feeling like you, Alix, that she was there all the time.'

'And of course it was she who made the birds tell us their stories,' said Alix, 'so we really should be very much obliged to her. Just think what nice games we've made out of them; and what nice things we've begun to get ready for the poor children next Christmas. I do think, Rafe, we've *never* felt dull since we've played so much in the Ladywood garden.'

Rafe quite agreed with her, and they made their way down the lane and through the well-known old gateway. It was the first time they had been in the deserted grounds so late of an evening. For they had had tea long ago, and it was not so *very* far off bedtime: already the bushes and shrubs began to look shadowy and mysterious in the twilight, and the moon's profile—for it was about half-way to full—to gleam pearl-like up among the branches.

'We mustn't stay very long,' said Rafe.

'Nurse won't mind our being a little later than usual, as she's busy packing,' said Alix. 'And it's still so hot, indoors at least. Last night I *couldn't* get to sleep, though I pushed off everything except one sheet. I was just boiling. And when I told mamma she said it was no use going to bed only to toss about, and that we might as well sit up a little later.'

"THEY BOTH STOOD STILL AND LOOKED."

' I hope it will be cooler at the seaside,' said Rafe.

' It's pretty sure to be,' Alix replied.
' If it was just about as cool as it is
here just now. Isn't it lovely? And
that breeze is so refreshing.'

They were standing near the walled-
up mound as she spoke, and the wind
came with a long sighing sound
through the trees. It seemed at
first like a sigh, but by degrees it
changed into a soft kind of laughter,
which did not fade away, but grew, as
they listened, more and more distinct.
And then it sounded as if coming not
from up among the trees overhead, but
from somewhere underground. And it
was not the wind after all, for by this
time everything was perfectly, strangely
still. The children looked at each
other; they were used to odd things
happening in the garden. They just
stood still and waited to see what was
going to take place.

The laughing ceased, and there

came a voice instead, and the voice
grew clearer as the hidden door in the
wall which they had sought for so often,
swung round, and out from the dark
passage came the small figure, red
cloak, hood, and all, of Mrs. Caretaker. She was still laughing just
a little, and her laugh was so bright
and rippling that it made the children
laugh too, though they did not know
why.

'And so you are going away, my
dears,' said their old friend. How she
got up so quickly to where they stood
they did not see, but there she was,
as alert as possible. And again she
laughed.

'If you please, if it's not rude, we'd
like to know what you're laughing at,'
said Alix, not quite sure if she was
pleased or not.

'Only a little joke, my dear; only
a little joke I was having all to myself.
I hear so many funny stories, you see.
They all have to tell me them : the

wind and the rain often chatter to me, as well as the birds and the bees and all the others that *you* call living creatures. And the sea, ah! the sea has grand stories to tell sometimes.'

'We're going to the seaside,' said Rafe.

Mrs. Caretaker nodded.

'I know,' she said, 'I know most things about my friends. I thought you would come to say good-bye before you left. I've been waiting for you. And if there is anything you would like me to take care of for you while you're away, you have only to tell me.'

'Thank you,' said the children. But Alix did not feel quite pleased yet.

'Mrs. Caretaker,' she said, 'you shouldn't speak as if this was the only time we've come to see you. We've been and been *ever* so often, but we never could find the door. And we've always kept saying how kind you'd been ; making the birds tell us stories too.'

'It's all right, my dear,' said the old woman. 'Yes, I heard you on the other side of the wall. But I'm very busy sometimes; too busy for visitors. I'm not busy to-night though, and it's getting chilly out here. Come inside with me for a while, and tell me about where you're going to.'

'We mustn't stay long,' said the children. 'It's later than usual for us to be out, but it's been so hot all day; we got leave to stay a little longer.'

'I will see you home. Don't be uneasy,' said Mrs. Caretaker. She led the way to the wall—almost without her seeming to touch it, the door opened, and they followed her along the little passage into the kitchen.

The fire was pleasantly low; the curtains were drawn back, and through the open window the moonlight, much clearer and fuller than in the garden outside, fell on a little lake of water, where two or three snow-white swans were floating dreamily. Rafe and

Alix almost screamed with surprise, but Mrs. Caretaker only smiled.

'You didn't know what a view I had out of my window,' she said, as she seated herself in her rocking-chair, and drew forward two stools—one on each side for the children. 'Yes, it is beautiful with the moon on it; and to-morrow night you will be looking at a still more beautiful sight— the great sea itself.'

'Do you love the sea?' they asked.

'Sometimes,' Mrs. Caretaker replied.

'You said it told you stories,' said Alix. 'Will you tell us one of them? Just for a treat, you know, as we are going away, and we can think of it when we are walking along the shore watching the waves coming in.'

Mrs. Caretaker did not speak for a moment.

Then she said—and her voice sounded rather sad—'I can't tell you one of the stories the sea tells me.

They're not of the laughing kind, and
it's best for you to hear them for
yourselves when you are older. But
I will tell you a little story, if you
like, of some of the folk that live in
the sea. Did you ever hear tell of
mermaids?'

'Oh yes!' cried the children, eagerly;
'often. There are lovely stories about
them in some of our fairy books; and
when we are at the seaside we do *so*
wish we could see them.'

Mrs. Caretaker smiled.

'I can't promise you that you ever
will,' she said; 'but you shall have my
story. Yes; sit closer, both of you,
and rest your heads on my knees.'

'You're not knitting to-night,' said
Alix. 'The last time the needles
made us hear the story better somehow; it was like as if you took us
a long way off, and the story came so
clear and distinct.'

'It will be all right, never fear,' said
the old woman. And as she spoke,

she gently stroked the children's heads.
Then the same strange feeling came
over them ; they felt as if they were
far away ; they forgot all about its
being nearly bedtime and about going
away to-morrow ; they just lived in the
story which Mrs. Caretaker's clear voice
began to tell.

'It is called

'THE MAGIC ROSE,'

said she ; 'but it is a story of those
that live in the sea. Down, deep
down below the waves, all is calm
and still, and there is the country
of the mermen. Strange things have
happened before now down there
among the sea-folk. Some who have
been thought drowned have been
cared for there, and lived their lives
long after those who had known them
up above were past and gone. For
the mer-folk are long-lived ; what men
count age is to them but youth ; their

days follow each other in a calm that
human beings could scarce imagine.
They live now in these stirring times
as their forbears lived when men and
women had their homes in the forests,
long before there were houses or towns,
or roads, or any of the things which
you now think the commonest neces-
sities.

But the sea-folk have their troubles
too, sometimes ; and my story has to
do with trouble.   The Queen — the
beautiful Queen of the sea-country
— was ill, and the King was in
despair.   Now I must tell you that
the Queen was not quite one of
the sea race — so at least it was
believed.   Her grandmother — or her
great - grandmother, maybe — was a
maiden of the land, who had fallen
into the sea as a little baby, and had
been brought back to life and cared
for by the mer-folk ; and when she
grew up, a great lord among them
loved her for her beauty and made

her his bride. She had no memory
of her native land, of course; but
still there were strange things about
her and her children, and their children again, which told whence they
had come.

And now that the young Queen
was so ill, one of these old feelings
had awakened.

'I shall die,' she said. 'I shall
surely die unless I can smell the
scent of a rose—a deep-red rose,
such as the land maidens love. It
has come to me in my dreams.
Though I have never seen one, I
know what it must be like, and I
feel that life would return—life and
strength that are fast fading away—
if I could breathe its exquisite fragrance and bury my face among its
soft petals.'

They were amazed to hear her speak
thus. The great court physicians at
first said she was wandering in her
mind, and no attention should be paid

to her.　But she kept on ever the same entreaty; and the King, who loved her devotedly, at last could bear it no longer.

'It all comes of her ancestor having been so foolish as to wed a human bride,' said one of the doctors, feeling in a very bad temper, as they all were.

The sea-doctors are not very wise, I fear, because they have so very little experience.　It happens so rarely that any of the mer-folk fall ill.　And so, as they had nothing to propose, the most sensible thing to do was to get angry.　But the King was not to be so put off.

'Whatever it comes from,' he said, 'I am determined that the Queen's wish shall be complied with if it is in any way possible.　What is this thing she is longing for?—what is a rose?'

The doctors did not know; but seeing that the King was so much

in earnest they agreed that they would
try to find out. And after a great
deal of consultation together, and
looking up in their learned books,
they did find out something. The
Queen, meanwhile, soothed by her
husband's promise that all was being
done to carry out her entreaty, grew
a shade better; at least for some
days she did not get any worse, which
was always something. And on the
fourth day the wise men asked for
an audience of the King in order to
tell him what they had discovered.

The King awaited them eagerly.

'Well,' he said, 'have you found
out what the Queen means by a
rose? And if so, how is one to be
procured?'

Yes; they were able to describe
pretty well what a rose was; for of
course, down below, they are not without gardens and flowers, though of
very different kinds from ours. But
a great difficulty remained. Even if

any one was daring enough to swim up to the surface and venture on land in search of the flower, and even if it was procured, how could it be brought, alive and fragrant, to the Queen?

'Why not?' asked the King. For he had never been up to the surface of the sea. It is one of the sea-people's laws that their royal folk must stay down below, so he knew nothing of the land or the things that grow there.

The learned men explained to him that, without air, and exposed to the salt water of the ocean, a flower of the earth must quickly fade and die; and as the King listened, his face grew sadder and sadder. But after a few moments' silence, one of the doctors spoke again. They were never in a hurry, you see, and they felt that it added dignity to their words to dole them out sparingly.

'It has occurred to us,' he said,

'that it might be well to consult the wise woman of the sea—the ancient mermaid who lives in the Anemone Cave. Not that as a rule, the advice of a member of her sex is of much use, but the ancient mermaid has lived long and——'

'Of course! of course!' exclaimed the King, impatiently; 'she is the very person. Why did I not think of her before? Why—the story goes that she nursed the Queen's human ancestress when, as a baby, she came among us.'

'I wish she had stayed away,' muttered the wisest of the wise men, though he spoke too low for the King to hear.

Then the King ordered his chariot and his swiftest steeds—they were dolphins—to be got ready at once, and off he set.

It was rather a long swim to the Anemone Cave. I wish I could give you any idea of the wonderful things

the King passed by on his way—the
groves of coral and forests of great
branching seaweeds of all shapes and
colour, the strangely formed creatures
whom he scarcely glanced at.   For of
course it was not wonderful to him,
and to-day his mind was so full of his
trouble that he would have found it
difficult to notice or admire anything.

The wise woman of the sea was at
home.   The King's heart beat faster
than usual as he was ushered into her
presence, not from cowardice, but because he was feeling so very anxious
about his dearly-loved wife.   And
King though he was, he made as low
an obeisance before the ancient mermaid as if he had been one of the
humblest of his own subjects.

She was very strange to behold.
Mermaids, as your stories tell you, are
often very beautiful, and possibly this
aged lady may have been so in her
day, but now she was so very old that
she looked like the mummy of a mer-

maid ; her hair was like a thin frosting
of hoar on a winter morning ; her eyes
were so deep down in her head that
you could scarcely see them ; the scales
on her tail had lost all their glitter.
Still there was something dignified
about her, and she received the King
as if quite prepared for his visit. She
was not the least surprised. Very wise
people, whether on land or in the sea,
never are, and she listened to the
King's story as if she knew all about
it.

‘Yes,’ she replied, in a thin croaking
voice like a frog's, ‘you have done well
to come to me. When the human
baby, the great-grandmother of the
Queen, was confided to my charge, I
studied her fate and that of her de-
scendants. The sea-serpent was an
admirer of mine in those days, and he
was very obliging. He noted the position of the stars when he went up
above, and reported them to me. Between us we found out some of the

future.   I read that a descendant of
the stranger should be seized with
mortal illness while still young, and
that her life should only be saved by
the breath of an earth-flower that they
call the rose, but that great difficulties
would attend the procuring it for her,
and that some conditions attach to the
matter which I was unable to understand fully.   All I know is this, the
flower must be sought for by a beautiful
and youthful mermaid, but the first
efforts will not succeed.   Now you
know all I have to tell you.   Farewell,
you have no time to lose.'

And not another word would the
wise mermaid say.

The King had to take leave.   His
dolphins conducted him home again
still more quickly than they had brought
him, for the words rang in his ears,
'You have no time to lose.'   Yet he
knew not what to do.   The conditions
he had already been told were difficult
enough, for it was not a very easy task

to swim to the surface, as, calm though
the ocean always is down below in the
sea-folks' country, there is no telling
how stormy and furious it may be up
above. And for a young and beautiful
mermaid to undertake such an adventure would call for great courage. It
was quite against the usual customs of
the sea-people.

For the old stories and legends we
hear about troops of lovely creatures
seen floating on the water, combing
their hair and singing strange melodies,
were only true in the very-long-ago
days. Now that mankind has spread
and increased so that there are but
few solitary places in the world, few
shores where only the sea-gull and the
wild mew dwell, the daughters of the
ocean stay in their own domain, whence
it comes that in these modern times
many people do not believe in their
existence at all.

The King went straight to the
Queen's bower, where she lay sur-

rounded by her ladies. She was sleeping, and though so pale and thin, her
face was very sweet and lovely, her
golden hair sparkling on the soft
cushions of sea moss on which she
lay. Even as she was, she was more
beautiful than any of the mermaids
about her.

Yet some of them were very beautiful.
The King's glance fell especially on two
who were noted as the most charming
among the Queen's attendants. Their
names were Ila and Orona. A sudden
idea struck the King.

'I will cause it to be announced
that a great reward shall be given to
any young and beautiful mermaid who
will undertake the quest of the red
rose on which depends the Queen's
recovery,' he thought, and the idea
raised his hopes. And as he stooped
over the sleeping Queen, she smiled
and whispered something as if she
were dreaming.

'The gift of love,' were the only

words he could distinguish. But he took the smile as a good omen.

The next morning there was great excitement amongst the fair young mermaids. For it was announced that whoever of them should succeed in bringing, blooming and fragrant, a red rose to the suffering Queen, should be rewarded by the gift of a pearl necklace, which was considered one of the most precious of the crown jewels, and that furthermore the fortunate mermaid should take the highest rank of all the sea-ladies next to the Queen herself.

Ila and Orona were both beautiful and courageous, and before the day was many hours older they had offered themselves for the task. The King was delighted, and as Ila was the elder of the two it was decided that she must be the first to try. She received many compliments on her daring, and the King thanked her most warmly. She accepted all that was said to her, but to Orona, who was her chosen confidante, she owned that she would never have dreamt of making the attempt but for her intense wish to possess the necklace, which she had often admired on the young Queen's fair skin.

'I would do anything to win it,' she said. 'There is nothing in the world I admire so much as pearls, but if I gain it, Orona, I promise to lend it to you sometimes.'

'Many thanks,' Orona replied, 'but I do not care for jewels as you do. If *I* have the chance of seeking the rose— that is to say if you fail—my motive will not be to gain the necklace, but to win the position of the highest rank next to the Queen. *That* I should care far more for.'

Both mermaids, however, kept their ambitions secret from every one else, and calmly accepted the praises showered upon them.

And the very next day Ila started on her upward journey.

CHAPTER XI

THE MAGIC ROSE (*continued*)

ILA found it trying and toilsome, for she was not accustomed to swimming upwards so long together, and she did not like to lose time by resting on the way. But when at last she reached the surface, her surprise at all she saw there took away her fatigue. It was a lovely summer day, the sunshine was deliciously warm, and as the mermaid lay on some smooth rocks a little way from the shore she could see the green fields, and trees, and houses, and gardens bordering the coast, quite

plainly.   She could even perceive some
people walking along, and she thought
their way of moving most extremely
awkward and ungraceful.

'Thank goodness I am a mermaid
and not a woman,' she thought.   'I
cannot believe that anything to be
found on land is as beautiful as our sea-
treasures.   How splendid the great
pearls in the centre of the necklace
would look in this brilliant light ! When
they are mine I must carry them up
here some day for the sake of seeing
them glisten on my neck in the sunshine.'

And her thoughts were so full of the
jewels that she almost forgot what she
had come for.   Suddenly the sight of
some red blossoms on a tree growing
close to the water's edge reminded her
of what she was there to do, and she
looked about her wondering how best
to set to work.   The wise men had
described roses to her ; they had even
found a picture of one in a book about

the plants of the land, so she knew very
fairly well what it should be like and
that it must have a delicious scent.
But that was all, and though she saw
fields and gardens not far off, she knew
not how to get to them. Suddenly
glancing in another direction she caught
sight of a barge, its white sails gleaming like the wings of a great bird, at
anchor some little way from the shore.
To and from this barge little boats were
coming and going, laden with baskets
and cases. Ila swam quietly towards
it, taking care to keep almost entirely
under water, so that she should not be
seen.

When she got quite close to the
barge she saw that one of the little boats
was approaching it, and this boat was
filled with flowers and rowed by but one
boy. The little vessel was in fact preparing for a pleasure trip, and the boats
were employed in bringing all that
could be wanted of decorations and
provisions. The boy rowed quite close

to the barge, and then throwing a rope on deck from his boat, he himself sprang on board to call some one to help him to unload his flowers.

Now was the mermaid's chance— she swam up to the boat and stretching out her hand drew from a basket, filled with roses of all shades, the most beautiful red one she could see. She had no doubt of its being a rose, for the perfume had reached her even some little way off. The boy turned round at that moment and gave a cry of terror as he caught sight of a shining white arm and hand taking a flower from the basket of roses, and for long after, a story went about that the spirit of some one shipwrecked off that coast haunted that part of the bay.

But Ila only laughed at the boy's fright, and swam off as fast as she could, delighted to have succeeded. She hid the rose carefully in the folds of the gauzy robe she wore, and after one breath of its fragrance prepared to

hasten home as fast as she could
go.

'The pearls are mine,' she thought
with exultation, giving no thought to the
poor Queen. 'I can fancy already that
I feel their smooth touch against my
skin—so adorned I shall certainly be
the most beautiful mermaid that has
ever been seen.'

But alas for vain Ila's hopes!

No sooner had she reached the
bottom of the sea than she hastened to
the palace, and sought at once for an
audience of the King. Eager past words
for her return, he hurried out to the
hall where she stood.

'I have got it,' she exclaimed, and
she slid her hand into the folds of her
dress and drew out—a little crumpled
rag—a few miserable leaves, sodden and
colourless, with no scent or fragrance—
the poor wretched ghost of what had
once been a magnificent rose!

The King's face fell. Ila gave a cry
of despair.

'I brought it so carefully,' she said.

'Your care was in vain,' replied the King. 'It is evident that some condition has not been complied with. How did you get the rose?'

She told him all, and Orona, who had followed her, listened eagerly.

'It may be,' said the King, 'that you took it without paying for it. I wish I had thought of that.'

But his hopes revived when he remembered that the 'first effort was not to succeed.' And too anxious to give much thought to Ila's disappointment, he turned to Orona.

'Now,' he said, 'it is for you to try. But you must take with you payment.'

'Yes,' said Orona calmly, 'I have thought of that. I will select two or three of our most valuable shells, for I have been told that rare shells are greatly esteemed by the land-folk. I am not surprised that Ila has been punished for taking what was not hers without paying for it.'

She looked so calm and confident that the King felt as if she must succeed. It was too late to set off that day ; but the next morning Orona started. She was far more business-like than Ila ; when she reached the surface, instead of wasting time in dreaming about the pearl necklace, she swam round the bay as near the shore as she dared venture, peering about in all directions. And at last she came to a little creek, which worked its way into the land till it became a small stream, whose banks were bordered by trees. This the mermaid followed for some distance ; till, tasting the water, she found it had almost lost its briny flavour altogether. This startled her, for no sea-folk could live many hours in fresh water, and she began to think she must turn back. But just then she saw that a few yards farther on the stream turned suddenly ; and swimming still a little way, she discovered that here it entered a beautiful park, through which it wound its way till lost to view.

And close to where Orona now was, stood a pretty cottage, whose garden at the back sloped down to the water, and here were growing in profusion flowers of many kinds; among them roses, red, white, and all shades between. For this was the cottage of the gardener of the great house, and he liked to have choice specimens of the flowers he tended near his own home.

It was easy for the mermaid to choose and gather a beautiful rose, for no one was about, it being still what human beings call very early in the morning. Orona did so, selecting carefully a rose not too fully blown, and wrapping it in some large cool green leaves which she found growing on the bank. And there, just where she had plucked the flower, she laid down two magnificent shells, which she had brought, as payment.

In her calm way, quite as triumphant
as her sister mermaid had been, Orona
swam back with all possible swiftness.
She reached her own country without
misadventure, and, smiling confidently,
entered the great hall of the palace,
where the King was awaiting her with
intense eagerness.

'Success!' she exclaimed, as she
drew out her leafy parcel. The outside
looked green and fresh enough, but,
alas! inside there was only the same
miserable little bundle of colourless rags
as Ila had brought back the day before
—nay, of the two, to-day's withered
flower looked even less like a rose than
the former one!

Orona clenched her hands in rage ;
the King's face sank into utter despair,
for the Queen's state was considered
worse this morning.

'Alas, alas!' he cried, as he turned
away, 'it is hopeless.'

But among those who overheard his
words was one who was not satisfied

with feeling very sorry for the poor King.

This was a little mermaid named Chryssa. She was younger than Ila and Orona, and she was of far less exalted position; in fact, she was scarcely more than a little servant in the Queen's household. And probably no one would have spoken of her as beautiful if asked to describe her. But she *was* beautiful, nevertheless, and wonderfully sweet and loving; and the living being she loved the most in the world was the Queen. Of course, like every one else, Chryssa had heard all about the quest of the rose which was to cure the Queen; and now the thought struck her, could *she*, un-known to any one, try in her turn to bring the earth-flower fresh and fragrant which alone would have magic power to save her royal mistress's life? There seemed something lucky in being the *third* to try, 'and, at least,' thought Chryssa, 'it would be, so far as I am concerned, "the gift of love," as the poor Queen keeps murmuring.'

She determined to make the endeavour; and late that night, just for fear of being seen—though she was so insignificant a person that there was not much chance of her being missed —she set off. She was not by nature so strong or courageous as Ila and Orona; she knew very little, indeed, of anything but her own sea home, as she had been treated like a child, and had never heard the stories and descriptions of the world above, which were often related to entertain the Queen and her ladies. No wonder her poor little heart almost failed her through the long dark journey up to land. And at first when she reached the surface all was still as dark there as below. But as she lay there panting, almost doubting if she had done well to come, up above, over the land, there shone out a marvellous light, which at once filled her with hope and joy. It was the moon—slowly the silvery lamp glided out from behind the clouds, and the little mermaid almost cried aloud for joy.

'Oh, beautiful light,' she said, 'thank you for coming. Show me what to do; I will follow your guidance,' and a gleaming streak across the water shone out as if inviting her to follow it.

Swiftly the mermaid swam in the direction of the land, full in the glow of the light; and a girl—an earth-maiden—standing at her window in the summer night thought that she saw a vision, and scarce knew if she were awake or dreaming.

'It is late,' she thought. 'I must get to sleep or I shall be growing too fanciful.'

But before she lay down on her little bed she carefully unfastened a beautiful red rose which was pinned to her bodice and placed it in a glass of water, kissing it as she did so, for it was the first gift of her betrothed.

Poor Chryssa reached the shore; but though the moonlight still shone pale and pure and clear, it gave her no help. For the radiance was now spread all over the land; and before her there stretched a steep and rocky coast, beyond which—far off it looked to the mermaid—she could dimly see trees and bushes and some darker, harder form among them.

'It may be a house, such as the earth-folk live in,' she thought. 'And there perhaps these flowers they call roses are growing. But how am I to get there? and how should I find the flower if I were there?'

Still she must try. Slowly and painfully she drew herself some little way up the shore, catching hold of the stones with her hands; then she stopped to rest, and set off again. It was really not very distant, but to poor Chryssa it seemed terrible: she could only go a few yards at a time without resting. The night was far gone, the dawn at hand, when the little mermaid, gasping and exhausted, her tender hands bruised and bleeding, sank for the last time, unable to drag herself any farther, on a grass plot just below the window whence the young girl had seen her in the moonlight like a vision, floating towards the shore.

Hebe, for so the maiden was called, woke early, and after glancing at her rose, threw open the window and leant out to watch the sunrise.

'How lovely it is,' she thought, 'and how happy I am!' for her betrothal had only taken place the day before. 'Dear rose, I will keep you always—even when withered—always, till——'

But a low sob or wail, just below the window, startled her. What could it be? Leaning farther out, she saw at first nothing but a long tangle of shining hair covering some unseen object, for Chryssa's hair was like a golden cloak.

'What is it? Who is lying there?'

A faint voice answered—

'Oh, lady, I think I am dying! I have lain here all night, torn and bleeding, and none of my race can live many hours on land.'

Half-terrified at the strange words, but still more pitiful, Hebe hastened out. The window opened on to a little balcony, and steps led down to the garden. She would almost have been too frightened to approach Chryssa—for though there were old legends of mer-folk about that coast, generations had passed since any had actually been seen—but for the sweet expression in the little mermaid's face and eyes, dying though she seemed. This gave Hebe courage to go near her, and with the ointment and linen she quickly fetched, to bind up her cuts and bruises. Then Chryssa told her story in gasping words.

'If I could but live to take a rose to the Queen,' she said, 'I would not mind dying; though, for one of my race, life should last for full five hundred years, and life is very beautiful.'

'Alas!' said the earth-maiden, 'there are no roses in our garden, the soil does not suit them; and before I could procure one for you, you would die, I fear. But '—and she made a great effort—'I will do for you what I had thought I could never do but a few minutes ago. I will give you my own rose—the first gift of my best beloved.' And with the words, she ran back to her chamber and returned, the red rose fresh and blooming in her hand.

She kissed it as she gave it to Chryssa.

'Carry healing in your fragrance,' she murmured. And, strange to say, as a breath of its perfume reached the mermaid, she herself in some magical way began to revive. Her eyes sparkled as she blessed Hebe for her generous sacrifice.

'I feel,' she said, 'that the conditions are all fulfilled. My Queen
will be saved.'

But Hebe's eyes looked over the
fields to where the waves were lapping
the shore.

'The tide is coming in,' she said,
'you will not now have so far to go.
But I must help you. Clasp me
firmly round the neck, and I will
carry you to the nearest creek, where
already you will find the ocean water,
which is to you what this fresh, balmy
air is to us.'

And little Chryssa did as she was
told, and Hebe, lifting the light burden
in her strong young arms, carried the
daughter of the strange unknown race
of the sea as tenderly as if she had
been a fragile sister of her own. For,
after all, there was the greatest of all
bonds between them—love and self-
sacrifice in their hearts.

All went well. Chryssa reached
the sea-king's palace feeling stronger

and better than when she set out, and
the rose, too, seemed to have gained
fresh beauty and fragrance by its con-
tact with the waves. No sooner did
the almost dying Queen breathe its
perfume than her strength began to
return, and in a few hours she was
cured.

No reward would have been too
great for the King and Queen to
bestow upon the little mermaid; but
she asked for none save to be her
mistress's constant attendant.

They say—so, at least, the waves,
who told me the story, whispered—
that down in the ocean depths, somewhere in a wonderful palace, there
blooms still a flower of earth—a red
rose—endowed with a magic gift of
health and healing.

Mrs. Caretaker's voice stopped. For
a moment or two the children did not
move. Then she laid her hand gently
on their heads, and they lifted them.

'It is a lovely story,' said Alix, with a sigh of content. 'Do you think, dear Mrs. Caretaker, that *perhaps* we may see Chryssa some day when we are bathing?'

Mrs. Caretaker shook her head.

'At least we may *look* for her; perhaps she comes up to the shore sometimes—we *might* catch a peep of her face among the surf. You might send her a message by one of the fishes you know, Mrs. Caretaker.'

The old woman smiled.

But suddenly Rafe started.

'I was forgetting,' he said. 'Haven't we been here a great while? What *will* nurse say?'

'Never mind,' said their friend. 'Remember, I promised to see you home,' and again she stroked their heads.

And that was all that happened, till——

'You must be getting up, my dear; to-day you are going to the sea, remember,' sounded first by one little bedside and then by the other.

'Were we very late of coming in last night?' asked the children at breakfast.

'Not so very, I don't think,' nurse replied. 'But you see I can't tell exactly, as I found you both undressed and in bed fast asleep when I came up from my supper. You did give me a surprise.'

Rafe and Alix looked at each other and smiled. Nurse thought it was only that they were pleased at the trick they had played her.

.   .   .   .   .   .

The seaside visit was delightful. But before it came to an end a very unexpected thing happened. The children's father, who was a very clever man, was chosen for an important post out of England. It all came about in a great hurry, and Rafe and Alix have never since returned to the country house where, for most of the years of their life, they had been so happy. And all this time their home has been a long way off.

They often speak of Ladywood, and declare that when they come back to England they *must* go there and try to find the old caretaker again. But I almost hope they will not do so; for, I am sorry to say, Ladywood has been bought and all changed. A new house has been built at last on the site of the old one, and the foundations all opened out. I feel sure Mrs. Caretaker is no longer there.

Still, there is no saying but that Rafe and Alix may come across her again *some* day and *some* where.

THE END

Printed by R. & R. CLARK, *Edinburgh*